KILL SHOT

The DCI tackles organized crime in this English murder mystery

JOHN DEAN

THE BOOK FOLKS

Published by The Book Folks

London, 2020

ISBN 978-1-913516-24-6

www.thebookfolks.com

KILL SHOT is the eighth book to feature DCI Jack Harris. It can be enjoyed as a stand-alone or as part of the series. Details of the other books are available at the end of this one.

Prologue

The evening sun was beginning to sink slowly over the North Pennines as the man in the camouflage jacket scrambled up the slope. Once he had reached the top, he dropped onto his belly and stared out across the moor. He lay there for more than a minute, conscious of his heavy breathing after the long climb and with the fresh aroma from the heather filling his nostrils. Were it not for the deadly purpose of the task in hand, he mused idly, it would be a beautiful summer evening on the northern hills but he was about to destroy that. He did not care. This was business. He had a job to do. No sentiment allowed.

The man removed the binoculars from his rucksack and focused on the nest which the female hen harrier had constructed in a dip a couple of hundred metres ahead of him. He gave himself time to take in the bird and her two chicks then, after placing the binoculars on the ground, slid the high-powered rifle from his shoulder, lifted the sight to his eye and focused once more on the nest.

The man gave a grunt of satisfaction. He knew this feeling well. He'd been there so many times before. Secure the target, do the job and get out of there without anyone being able to identify him. He gave a thin smile. This was all too simple. Easy money.

Chapter one

No one took any notice of the balding man with the pencil-line moustache and the outmoded brown suit as he stood in the busy main concourse at Manchester Airport. He let his gaze range across the check-in desks as he pondered which destination to select for his flight. For the first time in his sixty-one years, George Matthews could afford to go anywhere he wanted. Eventually, his gaze alighted on the board for Tenerife but he shook his head. He'd been there with his wife but that was during his old life. This was the first day of his new life. A life without Esther. He knew that she would be frantic with worry when she realised that he had disappeared but he did not care. He had taken his opportunity to get out and Esther deserved whatever came her way. She would be amazed that he was at the airport, he thought; she had always accused him of lacking adventure as the decades turned love into disdain. Well, now he would show her.

He looked at the boards again. New York. He'd always fancied going there. Looked good on the television. Or Acapulco, that had always sounded intriguing. Exotic. George picked up his bag. Yes, he'd go to Acapulco. He smiled. By the time Lynton Jago realised that the financial advisor had spirited away the gang's money, he'd be long gone. Payback for all those years of contempt and hurled insults. They could finance his exciting new life. One million pounds could fund an awful lot of wine, women and song.

As George headed for the airline desk, he stopped walking, placed his bag on the ground and frowned. It was all very well to talk of wine, women and song but when had he actually engaged in any of them? He'd always been a moderate drinker. Esther had been the one who'd imbibed. The one who gave him the sharp edge of her tongue when she'd had one too many. Esther had also been the only woman with whom George had ever slept. And as for song… he shook his head: what on earth had he been thinking?

And what precisely would he do when he landed in Acapulco? More doubts crowded in on him. George did not know anyone in Acapulco. He didn't even know where it was, for God's sake. He had a vague thought that it might be in Mexico. And he'd never been good at making friends either. Esther had always been the outgoing one, the one who did the talking, the adventurous one. And they'd always been abroad together. George would have been just as happy with Blackpool but Esther saw it as her mission in life to broaden his horizons. As he stood in the airport, memories of past trips came flooding back – and they were not all bad. There had been good times as well, particularly in the early years. George gave a slight smile, almost without realising that he had done it. Esther was right; he was lacking in adventure.

The smile faded as another thought assailed him. What if Jago had already discovered that the money was missing? George had gambled that, with Jago in the Caribbean and distracted by his daughter's wedding, it would be at least a week before he discovered that the cash had gone. Standing there amid the hordes of passengers, George began to panic. He relaxed after a few moments. He'd covered his tracks well. The money had found its way into his account through a circuitous route that would be difficult to trace and he had explained his absence to Esther by telling her that he was going away on business. Fail to turn up tomorrow and she would know that something was wrong and would raise the alarm. George picked up his bag and surveyed the check-in desks again, if he was going to flee the country, he had to be on that plane tonight.

But the nagging fear would not leave him. What if he was wrong? What if Jago had worked it out already? What if he had sent the others to get him? What if they were watching the airport, waiting for him to make his move? What if they were closing in on him as he stood there? George glanced round nervously, seeking threatening faces in the crowd that was milling around the concourse. Would it always be like this? Looking over his shoulder? Terrified of his own shadow? He realised with a sudden sense of shock that he had been blinded to reality when the opportunity to misappropriate the money fell into his lap. Hadn't thought it through. George Matthews, International Playboy, with a million burning a hole in his back pocket and a glamorous jet set life in Acapulco? Who was he kidding? He saw two police officers strolling towards him.

'Excuse me,' he said. 'I'd like to report a crime.'

Chapter two

In the market town of Levton Bridge, Jack Harris approached the end of his talk to the local bird club. As the wall clock ticked past 8:30pm in the parish hall, the detective chief inspector's constant companions Scoot and Archie, mongrels both, lay by the window and snoozed in the pool of light afforded by the sunshine filtering through the half-drawn curtains. Ostensibly, the inspector was delivering a routine talk on bird of prey persecution because, in addition to his role overseeing CID, he was the area's police wildlife liaison officer. However, everyone knew why he was really there. Jack Harris was going to lay down the law.

'So,' concluded Harris, 'to the hen harrier that has produced two chicks in our area for the first time in eleven years. Although we are keeping the location of the nest secret from the wider public, you all know that it is on Hewby Moor, following fifteen years of failed nesting on the estate.'

'Yes, well, you can blame Henry Masterson for that,' said a voice.

'I am not here to get into that debate again,' said Harris. He knew who had spoken. Didn't need to look. 'It's been damaging enough, as it is.'

A ripple of murmured agreement ran round the room.

'Oh, come on,' said the voice. 'We all know what Henry Masterson has been up to.'

This time, Harris focused his attention on Pete Guthrie, a wiry man who was sitting three rows back. His black hair was balding, his neatly trimmed beard showed the first signs of grey and he was wearing a chunky green sweater despite the warmth of the evening. Harris was not surprised that he was the one to challenge him; Guthrie was the most outspoken of the club members. Now, he was on his feet, his eyes bright with fervour.

'Everyone knows that Masterson has had his estate workers destroy the nests for years,' said Guthrie. 'The man will do anything to protect his grouse. You say the police are tough on persecution, Jack, but what are you actually doing about it?'

'Supporting this club's surveillance of the nest for starters,' said Harris. 'In fact, after this, I'm going up to do my latest stint. And don't forget that we can only do that because Henry Masterson has granted us permission to go onto his land.'

'Bloody PR stunt,' said Guthrie with a snort of derision. 'He only did it because the gamekeepers missed the nest. He'll find a way to get the chicks once they've fledged, you mark my words.'

'Be that as it may be, I am here to remind you all that I don't want to hear anything more about people taking the law into their own hands. I may be a club member but I'm also a police officer. You would do well to remember that.'

Ten minutes later, with the meeting finished and the hall all but empty, Harris was chatting to the bird club chairman at the back of the room.

'I'm sorry about that, Jack,' said the chairman.

'You don't need to apologise for Pete Guthrie.'

'Nevertheless, I feel bad about it. There's so much ill feeling over this. Sometimes, I wish that the damned things had never nested here.' The chairman noticed Guthrie approaching. 'I'm sorry, Jack, but I can't face talking to the man.'

He departed the room, leaving just Harris and Guthrie in the hall.

'You've got to stop shouting your mouth off like that, Pete,' said Harris.

'Why should I?'

'Because you're doing damage to the club. Can't you see that?'

'Pha! Fair-weather naturalists! Happy to go to the talks but ask them to actually *do* something... there's only seven of the buggers who have agreed to watch the nest. It's pathetic. Direct action, that's what we need.'

'That's the last thing we want,' said Harris. 'One of the gamekeepers had his tyres slashed the other day. I take it you know nothing about that?'

Guthrie said nothing.

'And I also heard that you accosted the estate manager when he was out for a meal with his family at The Hillview Hotel,' said Harris. 'If you're thinking of pulling any more stunts like that, you and I are going to fall out big time.'

'Yes, but Henry...'

'I've heard it all before, Pete. Like I keep saying, give me the evidence and I'll do something about it. If you don't, Masterson will have you for slander. It could cost you thousands.'

Pete Guthrie stalked from the hall without replying.

Chapter three

George Matthews had been sitting on his own in the interview room at the airport for the best part of an hour and was growing increasingly uneasy as the wall clock ticked off the passing minutes. Realising that he had not finished his tea, he reached out for the mug but was not surprised to discover that the liquid was cold. He was just debating whether or not to get up and leave the room – after all, he was not under arrest – when the door opened and a burly dark-haired man in a dark suit and with a pronounced five o'clock shadow walked in.

'Mr Matthews, I presume?' he said. He placed the notepad he was carrying on the desk and sat down. 'I am sorry to keep you waiting.'

'It's been more than an hour,' said Matthews. He surprised himself with the demanding tone of his voice. 'It's not on, it really isn't.'

The man seemed surprised to encounter such defiance in the meek-looking man sitting at the desk. He produced a warrant card from his jacket pocket, which he slid across the table so that Matthews could read the name.

'My name is Detective Chief Inspector Ged Rutherford, head of the Greater Manchester Police

Organised Crime Unit. They had to find me on my evening off. You've not exactly confessed to nicking a couple of chocolate bars from a sweet shop, have you?' There was an edge to his voice as the detective fixed Matthews with a steely glare. 'And I do hope that you're not wasting my time, sunshine.'

'I'm not.'

'You'd better not be.' Rutherford continued with his stern look. 'I was having a meal out with my wife. It's the first time we've been able to get out in weeks and she's well hacked off, so this had better be good.'

All the defiance of a few seconds drained away from George Matthews and he looked anxious. Rutherford suspected it was his default expression.

'So,' said the DCI, 'you claim to have stolen a million pounds from Lynton Jago, do you? Can I be absolutely clear about this before we go any further, we *are* talking about the gangland boss? This isn't some kind of misunderstanding, is it? Because if it is, I might just get back in time for the cheese board.'

'There's no misunderstanding.'

'I was afraid you'd say that,' said Rutherford with a sigh. 'So much for the port and Stilton. You do realise that you've consigned me to the spare room again, I take it? Look, Mr Matthews, with all due respect, why on earth would a man like Lynton Jago want to let you anywhere near a million quid of his money?'

'To invest. I believe that they call it money laundering.'

The ugly phrase seemed innocuous coming out of his mouth and there was a gleam in Rutherford's eye as he heard it. To his surprise, the DCI found himself convinced by the little man. He tried to appear calm, as if what he was hearing was of little import, but inside he was struggling to contain his excitement at the opportunity with which he had been unexpectedly presented.

'How long has this been going on then?' asked Rutherford. He fished a pen out of his jacket pocket and made a couple of notes. 'This money laundering?'

'Mr Jago first approached me four years ago.'

'And how much have you invested for him in that time?' asked Rutherford.

'Five and a half million pounds.'

Rutherford looked up from his notepad and stared at Matthews in amazement.

'Five and a half million?' he said. 'Are you sure?'

'I'm a very precise man when it comes to money, Chief Inspector. If you wish to be even more precise, I have invested five point six million for him. Mostly in emerging economies. South America, the BRIC countries, the Far East, that sort of thing. Technologies mostly. Not that Mr Jago is interested where the money goes as long as it makes him a good return.'

'And I am assuming that it does?'

'It does, yes. It's fair to say that I have added considerably to Mr Jago's wealth.'

'But why you?' asked Rutherford. 'With all due respect, you don't strike me as the criminal type.'

'He said he had heard that I was trustworthy.'

'And did you know who he was when he approached you?'

'Not at first.' George Matthews gave a slight smile. 'We tend to move in different circles, myself and Mr Jago. Oddly enough, he is not in my branch of Rotary.'

'I'm sure he's not.' Rutherford also gave a slight smile. 'He's probably ripped half of them off. So, when did you realise who he was?'

'After a couple of months,' said Matthews. 'There was a story in the newspaper saying that the police had interviewed him after the body of a man was found in the canal.'

Ged Rutherford thought back to the rainswept winter's morning when the body was discovered. He had been summoned to the banks of the Manchester Ship Canal following a tip-off to police about a body in a car. Rutherford recalled how he had stood shivering on the towpath and watched as the recovery truck winched the Fiat out of the water. He had moved in closer as officers prised open the boot of the vehicle to reveal the trussed-up body of a man with a neat bullet hole in the centre of his forehead. A man who it later emerged had crossed Lynton Jago – not that the police were ever able to prove anything.

'I was horrified,' said Matthews.

'But not horrified enough to stop working for him?'

'You don't say no to a man like Lynton Jago, Chief Inspector. Not unless you wish to end up in the boot of your car like that poor man did.'

Rutherford looked across the table at George Matthews.

'No,' he said. 'No, I don't imagine that you do.'

Chapter four

The two men sitting on the moor overlooking the hen harrier's nest had finished their tea and Geoff Morden, a swarthy, well-built man, nodded at his friend's mug.

'Top up?' he asked. He reached into his bag and produced a half-full bottle of whisky. 'Perhaps something a little stronger this time?'

'Now there's a good idea,' said Harry Groves, a man in his mid-forties, his face weather-beaten from a life spent outdoors as a fisheries inspector. 'Mind, only the one. It *is* Jack Harris taking over from me.'

'Do you really think Jack will mind if you've had a couple of snifters?' asked Morden. He poured the drinks. 'Take it from me, he's done the same in his time. And worse.'

'I guess so.'

Morden glanced at his watch.

'When is he taking over from you?' he asked.

'Tennish,' said Groves. 'Depends how long the talk goes on.'

'By which, read how long Pete Guthrie is on his feet,' said Morden with a sly smile. 'He's really gunning for Jack, is Pete.'

'More fool him then. You don't want to cross Jack Harris.'

'I tried telling him that, but he wouldn't listen.'

* * *

Lying on the opposite slope, concealed by the heather, the gunman nestled the rifle in the crook of his shoulder.

Having scrutinised the hen harrier nest through the rifle sight, the gunman switched his attention to the men on the far slope. Screwing up his eye to see better, he could make out that, as expected, there were two of them. They were sitting on folding chairs that had been erected in front of a small green tent and he could see that they were drinking from mugs and talking, although they were too far away for him to hear their voices, even on such a still summer evening. The gunman returned his attention to the nest.

He felt his trigger finger tense, held still for a moment to be sure of his aim, then squeezed. The bullet slammed into the ground a couple of feet from the nest, spitting up clods of soil and startling the birds. Before the men guarding the nest could react, the gunman had swung the weapon round and fired again.

Chapter five

Having left the parish hall, Jack Harris loaded the dogs into the back of his mud-spattered, white Land Rover and started the journey to the nest site. He had just guided the vehicle out of Levton Bridge and was looking forward to the drive along the sunlit moorland road when the radio crackled into life. A woman's voice came over the airwaves.

'Urgent message for DCI Harris,' said the control room operator. 'Detective Inspector Roberts asks if you are able to attend a shooting on the Hewby Moor Estate?'

'Hewby Moor?' said Harris. 'Are you sure?'

'That's the location we have, sir.'

'Where's it happened? The house?'

'Negative, sir. The location has been given as the hen harrier nest site. DI Roberts said that you would know where that is. The caller reports one fatality.'

Jack Harris had an overwhelming sense that he knew who the victim was, that it was all too late for him and Geoff Morden. Time had run out on his attempt to get close to the man again. Too many things would be left unsaid. The inspector felt a knot forming in the pit of his stomach but attempted to sound casual as he replied, trying to conceal from the control room operator the growing sense of dread that he was experiencing. If he was right, it threatened to complicate things.

'Do we have a name for the dead person?' he asked.

'The caller said that it's Geoff Morden. He said you'd know him.'

Harris closed his eyes for a couple of seconds as confirmation triggered a rush of memories, memories that had been particularly powerful since Morden's return to the valley a few weeks previously. Memories of times long gone, of another age before their lives took them in different directions. After a few moments, the inspector remembered that he was driving and opened his eyes.

'Are you still there, sir?' asked the control room operator.

'Yes, I'm here. Sorry. Who called it in?'

'Harry Groves. They were watching the nest together, apparently.'

'They were, yes. Are uniform on the way?'

'They are, yes.'

'Mark me in attendance as well then,' said Harris.

'DI Roberts said to tell you that the gunman has not yet been apprehended so you need to be careful. She says you might want to call her before you get there. She's helping to co-ordinate the search operation.'

'Will do.'

He ended the conversation and pressed hard on the accelerator and the Land Rover jolted forward. As he drove, he allowed the memories to crowd in. Golden memories of long summer days, of two teenage friends roaming far and wide over the northern hills from dawn until dusk, young men free of cares, full of life and laughter, with their dogs at their heels and the future at their feet with little insight into what it might hold. He frowned as the happy memories were replaced by darker ones: confrontations with the police, raised voices between friends, the conflict that forced the teenaged Harris to sever his friendship with Geoff Morden and leave him and the others behind to travel the world with the Army.

The most recent memories were equally conflicted, two middle-aged men attempting to overcome the awkwardness caused by so many years without seeing each other. And all with Harris concealing his true intentions from his old friend. Harris decided not to think about it. Not until he knew if there was a connection between his covert inquiries and the shooting.

Keeping one eye on the road, Harris reached across to scroll down the contact list on his mobile phone, which was sitting in its cradle on the dashboard. He stopped at the name Gillian Roberts, Levton Bridge's Detective Inspector, the organiser, the mother-of-two whose carefully cultivated matronly demeanour masked a mind as sharp as they came. The right person to have on your side in a crisis. He punched in the number.

'Gillian, it's me,' he said when the call was answered. 'I'm on my way to Hewby Moor. What's happening?'

'Not quite sure yet, Hawk.' The detective inspector's voice was as calm as ever, but he could sense anxiety lurking behind it. 'I'm still trying to make sense of things. All we've got is Harry Groves' account to go on.'

'Where is he?'

'He's staying with the body until we arrive, but when I rang him a few minutes ago, he wasn't sounding great. I suspect that he's going into shock.'

'What do we know?'

'Just that someone took a couple of pot-shots at the hen harrier nest and that one of them missed and struck Geoff Morden. You OK to take this one given your friendship? I mean, if it's too close to home I can always…'

You have no idea, thought Harris.

'No, it's fine,' he said. 'Thanks for the offer, though. Any word on the gunman?'

'Harry lost sight of him and we have no idea where he is now. Uniform are on their way up there but God knows what they can do at this time of day. It'll be dark soon.'

'What about the helicopter?' asked Harris. 'It has thermal imaging equipment.'

'It's also grounded for routine maintenance.'

'Shit, I forgot that. Any others we can pull in?'

'I've already submitted the request.'

The Land Rover's tyres squealed as the inspector hurled the vehicle round a tight bend.

'Any description of our guy?' he asked.

'Just that he was wearing dark trousers and a camouflage jacket. Harry says he didn't recognise him but he was quite a distance away. Said he was heading east across the moor on foot.'

'OK, I'll ring you when I meet up with uniform,' said Harris as he negotiated another bend at speed.

'Head for the track that runs not far from the nest site. Charlie Gates is running things. And be careful.'

'Always,' said Harris.

He ended the call and pulled the Land Rover over to the side of the road, where he sat in silence for a few moments. God, how he hoped the death was an accident. The inspector scrolled down his smartphone's contact list and stopped at a name which consisted only of the letter P. He hesitated for a moment, sighed and dialled the number.

'Jack,' said a woman's voice. He could just make out soft music playing in the background.

'I hope I'm not disturbing anything, Susan.'

'No, it's fine. What can I do for you at this hour?'

'Geoff Morden is dead.'

There was silence for a few moments.

'That complicates things,' said the woman. 'How did he die?'

'You know that nest he was guarding? Well, it looks like someone took a pot-shot at the birds and hit him by accident.'

'You sure it's an accident?'

'It's what it looks like.'

'When will you know for definite?' she asked.

'I'm on my way up there at the moment but I'm going to have to reveal what I know, aren't I? I mean, now that he's dead.'

'Not if it's an accident, you won't,' she said. 'If it's an accident, nothing changes. Nobody needs to know anything. No connection.'

'But…'

'Just act as you would normally and ring me in the morning.' The voice suggested finality.

Harris concluded the call and frowned. He knew that he shouldn't have taken on the job for her. Too many competing loyalties. He slipped the Land Rover into gear and resumed his journey. The light was fading rapidly as, fifteen minutes later, the inspector edged the vehicle along the rough track which ran across the moorland a mile from the nest site. The headlights glowed brightly in the gathering gloom. Ahead were more lights and the inspector pulled up next to a couple of police patrol cars. Ordering the dogs to stay in the vehicle, Harris got out, took his Barbour jacket off the passenger seat and walked up to the uniformed inspector, who was talking to a couple of officers.

'What we got, Charlie?' asked Harris.

'Not sure yet, Jack. We've only just got here ourselves.' Charlie Gates gestured to the sky. 'One thing's for sure. We are going to lose the light soon.'

'What's your plan?'

'Top priority is to get Harry Groves down safely. An ambulance is on its way.' The inspector held up his forefinger as he heard the distant wail of a siren carried on the still night air. 'Ideally, I'd like to send them straight up but I'm worried when we have a lunatic running round with a gun. I've got the mountain rescue guys on standby to recover the body as well but I'm loathe to send too many people up there at once until I know exactly what's happening.'

'Agreed. You called in firearms?'

'On their way. We're setting roadblocks up on the main routes out of the valley and they're going to put as many of their officers on them as they can. They're sending someone here as well.' Gates glanced at the darkening sky again. 'However, without the chopper I'm not that confident that we can find our guy tonight. There's loads of ways he could get past us.'

Harris nodded gloomily and stared out across the moor. As someone who had known the hills since childhood, he was familiar with the network of tracks and country lanes that weaved their way off the hills, bypassing the main roads. Few knew them better. The thought brought back memories of Geoff Morden again. The inspector tried to push them to the back of his mind.

'How's Harry?' he asked.

'Pretty shaken up,' said Gates. 'He needs someone with him ASAP, really.'

'I'll go.' Harris started to put his coat on. 'It's only a twenty-minute walk. Won't take me long.'

'You'll want to wait for the firearms officer, though? Just in case?'

'I don't like the idea of leaving Harry up there on his own any longer that we need to, Charlie. And it'll mean that I can check it out before you send the ambulance crew up.'

'But what if chummy comes back?'

'If he's got any sense, he'll be well away,' said Harris. 'I'll stay up there overnight as well. There's no way forensics can do anything tonight so we need to preserve the scene. It's not due to rain so it should be OK. I'd like to get Doc up here at first light so that he can see the body in situ. We'll need a quad bike or something to get him and his arthritic leg up there.'

'I've got officers on the way over to the estate office now. I'll get them to ask if they can spare one.' Gates frowned as Harris turned back towards his vehicle. 'You sure about spending the night up there, Jack? Sounds risky to me.'

'I'll be OK. I was supposed to be there, anyway, watching the nest. I don't suppose there's any news on the birds?'

'You and your blessed birds.' Gates gave a slight smile. 'I'm afraid that they're pretty low on my list of priorities at the moment.'

'I guess they are.' Harris gave him a rueful look. 'Isn't it always the way?'

''fraid so, old son.'

Harris walked over to the Land Rover and returned with a haversack on his back and his two dogs trotting eagerly at his heels.

'They'll be OK up there?' asked Gates doubtfully. 'Wouldn't want them to get shot.'

'What about me?'

'You can look after yourself.' Gates gestured to a couple of young constables standing by one of the patrol vehicles and staring nervously out across the moor. 'If you fancy some company, you could have one of the bairns.'

Harris surveyed their fresh-faced features without enthusiasm for a few moments. He'd been concerned about the young age of the recruits being sent to Levton Bridge for some time. He felt that his own CID team was too short of experienced officers and knew that the situation was little better in uniform.

'They're up to it?' he asked.

'Be good experience.'

'But for whom?'

Gates gave a low laugh.

* * *

Within a couple of minutes, Harris and one of the constables had started off across the moor. The inspector and the dogs walked with the sure and steady step of those who had spent many hours on the northern hills but the uniformed constable was less sure of his footing as he followed his torch beam to negotiate a way along the rough path, repeatedly stumbling as he struggled to keep up with the rapid pace being set. After they had walked in silence for five minutes and the other uniformed officers had faded from view behind them, Harris remembered his responsibilities and stopped to allow the young man to catch up.

'You're new, aren't you?' said the inspector. 'Not sure we've spoken, have we?'

'No, sir. Constable Jardine. Leslie Jardine.' The young constable was breathing hard after the exertion. 'I only transferred up from Roxham ten days ago.'

'Scared?'

Taken aback by the question, the constable did not reply immediately; if he was honest, he was more frightened of making a fool of himself in front of Jack Harris than he was of the gunman. Every new recruit at Levton Bridge Police Station had it drummed into them on day one that Harris was a man who did not suffer fools gladly. Or at all. The inspector noted his confusion and gave a slight smile; he knew what people said about him, and played up to the reputation. He decided to try to put the young man at ease. The last thing he wanted was a jittery officer if the gunman did reappear.

'I'd be surprised if you weren't scared,' said Harris. He started walking again. 'I sure as hell am.'

'You, sir?' Jardine stared at him in surprise.

'There'd be something wrong if I wasn't, don't you think, Constable? Just keep your eyes peeled.' Harris glanced across at the young officer and gave him a reassuring smile. 'You be OK?'

The constable nodded.

'I'm OK,' he said.

'Good lad.'

It took them a further fifteen minutes to reach the site. When they arrived, Harris flashed his torch in the direction of the nest and, having peered into the fading light for a few moments, was relieved to see that the female and her two chicks appeared to still be there. The officers gave the nest a wide berth and climbed the far slope where they found Harry Groves sitting next to the body of Geoff Morden, his hands shaking, his face pale and his eyes wide and staring. His thinning brown hair was slicked with sweat and he was rocking gently to and fro. Harris removed his coat and placed it round his shoulders.

'Boy, am I glad to see you,' said Groves. His voice trembled slightly.

'Got here as fast as we could.' Harris looked across at Morden, who lay on his back not far from the tent. Blood was still oozing from a wound in the chest. 'What the hell happened here, Harry?'

Groves turned haunted eyes on the detective.

'He just shot him,' he said in a hollow voice. 'Appeared from nowhere and shot him.'

'No warning?'

'Nothing.'

Harris gave Groves a few moments to compose himself, relieved to see that the officers' arrival had calmed him down slightly. The rocking had slowed and colour was returning to his face.

'And you think he was after the birds?' asked the inspector.

'What else could it be?' Groves pulled the coat tighter round him. 'The first shot damn near hit the nest. Perhaps he didn't see us.'

'You weren't exactly hidden from view, were you?' Harris glanced at the bottle lying nearby, its contents spilled. 'Sitting on the hillside drinking whisky. You didn't recognise him?'

'It all happened so fast, Jack.' Groves looked at the body and shook his head. 'What a terrible thing to have happened.'

Silence settled for a few moments then the young constable broke off from staring out across the moor to glance at Harris.

'Do you think he'll come back, sir?' he asked.

Harris flashed his torch into the constable's face and noted how the young man was looking increasingly uneasy. His expression reminded Harris of long nights spent on guard duty in the years after he left his beloved valley to join the Army, of the tricks that his mind used to play as he clutched his rifle and stared out into the shadows in search of movement.

'Probably not,' he said after a few moments. 'I'd get myself as far away from here as possible, if I was him. Wouldn't you?'

The constable nodded. The inspector fished his mobile phone out of his trouser pocket, was relieved to see that he had reception and dialled a number. The screen glowed brightly in the darkness.

'Charlie?' said Harris when the call was answered. 'Are the paramedics there yet?'

'Yeah, they arrived a couple of minutes ago. Am I OK to send them up?'

'Fine,' said Harris.

* * *

Several miles away, having made his way across the darkening moor, the gunman began to climb the slope leading to a copse, its trees bent and twisted after years of fierce North Pennines winds. On reaching the woodland fringe, he paused to catch his breath and glance back towards where he had come. Noticing the faintest pinpricks of light in the far distance, he tensed, slipped his bag off his shoulder and produced a pair of binoculars. Lifting them to his eyes, he peered in the direction of the nest site for a few moments and honed in on the lights. Unable to make anything out, even with night-sight, he returned the glasses to the bag and set off again with a quickening step, the step of a man who knew it was *job done* and that it was time to make himself scarce.

Chapter six

It was shortly after 11:00pm when there was a loud knock on the door of the interview room at Manchester Airport. George Matthews started and Ged Rutherford tensed. He was only too aware that, although they were in supposedly secure surroundings, their safety was far from guaranteed when it came to a man with a long reach like Lynton Jago. The more the detective had talked to the financial advisor, the more he had been overwhelmed by the enormity of what was at stake if what he was being told was true. And what Lynton Jago might do to keep it from reaching a courtroom.

Rutherford knew, however, that he still needed to be cautious when assessing what George Matthews was telling him because his credibility was still at stake a year after returning to the Organised Crime Unit following his promotion to DCI. Not for nothing had Lynton Jago managed to evade prison for so long and Rutherford was still experiencing nagging doubts about Matthews. It all seemed far too good to be true and Jago had made many a good detective appear impotent down the years. Sitting in the oppressive atmosphere of the cramped office, Rutherford recalled the frustration felt by Jack Harris when he was making his name leading the team that broke up a number of the gangs in the city. Rutherford remembered only too well the night when a frustrated Harris punched a hole in the office wall when he realised that Jago had slipped through their fingers again. The memory spoke to Ged Rutherford now.

There was a second knock on the door, more insistent this time, breaking into the inspector's reverie.

'Who is it?' asked Rutherford.

'Gerry,' said a voice from the other side of the door.

'Come in,' said Rutherford.

A plainclothes officer with tousled dark hair and wearing jeans and a leather jacket walked into the room.

'What is it?' asked Rutherford.

Detective Sergeant Gerry Bayliss looked at George Matthews and hesitated.

'You can speak in front of him,' said Rutherford.

'I've been looking at some of the airport CCTV,' said Bayliss. 'I'm pretty sure that I recognised two of Lynton Jago's men. They arrived twenty minutes ago.'

'What were they doing?'

'Scanning the departure queues, by the look of it. Oh, and I checked with the airline. Lynton Jago is booked on a plane back to the UK from the Caribbean tonight. He was supposed to be coming back on Tuesday but brought it forward. Made the booking earlier today and left his family there. Arrives at 6:00am.'

'Well, Mr Matthews,' said Rutherford. He noted that the colour had drained from the financial advisor's cheeks. 'I guess that answers one question. Lynton Jago would appear to *have* worked things out.'

And confirmed my big opportunity, thought the inspector. He tried not to think about the satisfaction that he would experience when Harris discovered that it was him who had locked up Lynton Jago.

'The bigger question,' said Rutherford, looking at Matthews, 'is what do we do with you now?'

'You promised me protection,' said Matthews plaintively.

'I haven't promised you anything yet.'

'But you said…'

'I said it depends entirely on what we can prove,' said Rutherford. 'All you've given me so far is a few general accusations but nothing to back them up. That's the story of my life when it comes to Lynton Jago. Now, if you can provide some evidence…'

'I keep telling you, I won't give you anything more unless I have protection,' said Matthews. 'I demand it.'

'Demand?' said Rutherford sternly. 'You are in no position to demand anything. To be honest, Mr Matthews, I haven't worked you out yet. Maybe you're just a bit part player of no use to us. Or perhaps you're a fantasist with a big mouth and a death wish. We've never heard of you, have we, Sergeant?'

Gerry Bayliss shook his head.

'Nope,' he said. 'And we know all the players in Jago's organisation.'

'But I'm telling you the truth,' said Matthews.

'But you can see our problem, can't you? Whenever I ask you for the evidence, you say you won't tell me where it is unless I guarantee you protection. Protection is expensive, Mr Matthews, and I have to be sure before I provide it. It's not easy persuading my bosses to pay for it, you know.'

Rutherford allowed a thin smile to play across his face.

'I don't know, Gerry,' he said as if he was thinking aloud. 'Maybe we should let him go for tonight. Let us all sleep on it. See you again in the morning. Talk it over then. What do you think?'

'Well, if he's not being co-operative…'

'You can't do that!' exclaimed Matthews. He looked at Bayliss in alarm. 'You heard what he said. Jago's men are here. If they find me, they'll kill me. You know what they're like.'

'Then I need to know where the evidence is and I need to know now.' There was steel in Rutherford's voice. 'My time is too precious to have it wasted with silly games. Deal or no deal?'

Defeated, Matthews nodded.

'I keep it in a locked drawer in the spare room at home,' he said quietly.

'Not at your office?'

'I work from home. You can have it all.' Tears started in Matthews' eyes. 'Just keep me safe. And Esther. I don't want anything to happen to her.'

'Ah, yes, Esther,' said Rutherford. 'And you say that she knows nothing about this?'

'Nothing.'

'In which case, if she's anything like my missus, I suspect that you should be more frightened of her than anyone sent by Jago. I'm sure she'd love to know why you were heading off without her.' Rutherford glanced at Bayliss. 'Take a bit of explaining, that will, eh, Sergeant?'

Bayliss grinned.

'Very well,' said Rutherford. He had got what he wanted. 'You've got your protection, Mr Matthews. You got someone watching the house, Gerry?'

'Yup. And I've got the rest of the team on standby.'

'OK, get the key from Mr Matthews and go and get the documents. And bring Esther in.'

'When will I see her?' asked Matthews.

'Tomorrow maybe. You'll be kept at different safe houses overnight and we'll talk to you again in the morning.' Rutherford nodded to Bayliss. 'Get him out of here but make sure that no one sees him go. And make sure that whoever takes him to the safe house has someone with them at all times. I suspect there's a lot of people who would like to talk to Mr Matthews. I don't want them trying to spring him.'

'Will do,' said Bayliss. He placed a hand on Matthews' shoulder. 'Come on, sunbeam.'

'I just hope you appreciate what you've done,' said Rutherford as the financial advisor stood up.

Matthews nodded unhappily.

'I suspect life will never be the same,' he said.

'At least you've still got a life. Not everyone who crosses Lynton Jago is that fortunate.' Rutherford knew that it was a cruel thing to say but he couldn't help himself. Something about the meek little financial advisor brought out the worst in him. 'I'd be thankful for small mercies, if I were you.'

The colour drained out of George Matthews' face again as a grinning Bayliss led him from the room.

Chapter seven

Days spent fighting organised crime in Manchester were a long way from Jack Harris's thoughts; he, Harry Groves and the young constable sat in silence for the best part of an hour as darkness enveloped the hills and they waited for the ambulance crew to arrive at the nest site. Although Harris had known Groves since they were children in the valley, the two men had never been close and neither of them spoke. Besides, each one of the three felt a growing sense of unease as the warmth of the day was replaced by the chill of the night. Each was acutely aware that, despite the inspector's attempts to strike an unconcerned note, the gunman could be watching. It was with relief that they spotted lights approaching slowly across the lower slopes and, after a few minutes, heard the sound of boots tramping on the heather and the low murmur of approaching voices.

Within a few minutes, the ambulance crew emerged from the darkness, accompanied by a uniformed officer with a gun slung across his back and followed by a balding man wearing a dark suit underneath a green anorak. The dogs rushed to greet the new arrivals and Harris nodded a welcome at the paramedics and the armed officer, who extended a hand of welcome.

'Davy Morrison,' he said. 'Firearms Unit.'

'Good to meet you, Davy,' said Harris as they shook hands. The inspector turned to the balding man. 'Matty, lad, didn't think I'd see you up here.'

'You know me, guv, just love the hills.' Detective Sergeant Matthew Gallagher gave his boss a rueful look. 'Absolutely bloody *love* them.'

Harris smiled. Everyone knew that Gallagher had only moved north from London because his wife wanted to be near her elderly parents and that, even after his years in Levton Bridge, the sergeant still struggled with life in the North Pennines.

Gallagher glanced across to the young constable, who was watching as the paramedics began to attend to Harry Groves.

'Besides,' he said in a low voice, 'Charlie Gates thought that you might like someone your own age to play with.'

'He's not been too bad.'

'I take it that you put him at ease with your natural easy-going charm then?' said the sergeant.

'Something like that.'

'Poor bastard.'

Both men smiled. They were very different personalities: Harris, born and bred in the valley, strong-jawed, thick brown hair without a hint of grey, the less talkative one; Gallagher, a decade younger, smaller, stocky, black hair starting to thin – a man, some said, with the appearance of a monk – the more forthcoming character.

'You planning to stay up here overnight?' asked Harris.

'That's the plan, yes. The DI thought you might appreciate some help when forensics arrive in the morning. Everything is covered at her end and she's sent Allison over to the estate office with some uniforms.' Gallagher looked at the young constable again. 'Charlie suggests that we send meladdo back down with the ambulance guys. Leave me and Davy up here with you.'

'Makes sense.' Harris gestured to the tent. 'You ever camped then?'

'Couple of times when I was a Boy Scout back in London. Only in Green Park, mind.' Gallagher looked around him gloomily. 'And there was a McDonald's nearby. Not sure I can see one here, though. Pity, I'd love a Big Mac.'

'Sorry. No Big Macs here. Any news on the gunman?'

'No one's gone through the roadblocks, apart from a few locals.' Gallagher glanced at the body of Geoff Morden. 'What on earth is this about, guv? I know people get aeriated about the birds but shooting someone? Can't see it, somehow.'

'Except that Geoff is one of Pete Guthrie's mates,' said Harris. 'They've been pushing their luck. Stirring things up.'

'Guthrie's a bit of a hothead, from what I hear,' said Gallagher. 'He's the one who threatened the estate manager and his family at The Hillview Hotel, isn't he?'

'Jeez,' said Davy Morrison. 'All over a few birds.'

'Hen harriers are different, though,' said Harris. 'Mention them to some people and the red mist comes down.'

'Enough to shoot someone?' asked Morrison.

'It could still be an accident,' said Harris. He glanced over to where the paramedics were attending to Groves. 'Harry is adamant that the first shot was aimed at the nest and it wouldn't be the first time that someone has tried to shoot hen harriers. There was a similar incident down in Yorkshire a few years back where a gamekeeper was fined.'

'So, it could well be one of the Hewby Moor gamekeepers then,' said Gallagher.

Harris did not reply and, for a fleeting moment, Gallagher sensed that his boss was uncertain about how to reply. It was something that he was unused to witnessing.

Harris was normally the most decisive of officers. In Gallagher's experience, it was what set DCIs apart as leaders. Before Harris could say anything, his mobile rang. He put the call on speaker so that the others could hear.

'Gillian,' he said. 'What's happening?'

'Alison has just been on from the estate office,' said Roberts. 'They're adamant that all their people are accounted for and that none of the gamekeepers have been out tonight. It seems to check out.'

'You track down Geoff's daughter yet?'

'Yeah, and you're right. She's still in Manchester. GMP are going to bring her up first thing in the morning. I said there was little point in doing it tonight. Oh, and we got the landlord to let us into Geoff Morden's rented house in Tenter Street but there was nothing out of place.'

'And the gunman?' asked Harris. 'Any news?'

'I have this awful feeling that he's slipped through the net.'

'So do I. Keep me informed.' Harris ended the call and watched as the paramedics began to lead Harry Groves away. 'He's going to be OK?'

'Bit shocked,' said one of the paramedics. 'We've given him something to calm him down and we'll get him checked out at Roxham General, just to be sure.'

'I'll make sure that someone takes you home from the hospital, Harry,' said the inspector. 'And we'll leave it until tomorrow to take a statement from you. When you're feeling better.'

Groves nodded his gratitude and the small group moved off down the slope. Once their torchlights had faded into the darkness, Harris disappeared behind the tent and re-emerged with several logs. Within a few minutes, and having judged that they were far enough away from the nest to avoid disturbing the birds, he had started a fire and the three officers gathered round it, warming their hands by the flickering flames.

Chapter eight

As the silence deepened on the moor, Matty Gallagher glanced at the body, which was vaguely visible in the shadows cast by the flickering light from the campfire. The sergeant was sitting on one of the folding chairs, Harris on the other with the dogs at his feet, and Davy Morrison was on the ground. Gallagher looked at Harris. The inspector was a brooding presence; distracted. He was never the most talkative of men but Gallagher sensed that this was something different.

'You OK?' asked the sergeant.

At first Harris did not appear to have heard then he nodded.

'Yeah, I'm OK,' he said. 'It's a bit different when you know them, isn't it?'

'Yeah, it is,' said Gallagher. 'When I was with the Met, one of the lads on my shift lost his son. Innocent bystander in a drive-by. We all knew the kid and it was one of the most difficult investigations that I have ever carried out, so I know what you are going through. You and Geoff Morden were close, I think.'

'Maybe once.'

Gallagher waited for the inspector to elaborate on the comment but he did not say anything. The sergeant knew to stay silent; although the two men had grown close over the years, he had never found Harris particularly forthcoming when it came his personal life. Things had been improving gradually since the inspector had started a relationship with Jenny Armannsson, head of the fraud squad at Greater Manchester Police, but Harris still only discussed his personal life on his own terms.

'You don't have to tell us, if you don't want to,' said Gallagher as the silence lengthened. 'I mean, if it's too close to home to–'

'No, it's alright.'

'So, what's the story then?'

'A long one.'

Gallagher stared into the darkness.

'We seem to have plenty of time,' he said.

Harris paused for a few moments. *Just act as you would normally*. He knew that it would only arouse suspicions if he remained silent but resolved to tell the others only what they needed to know. After all, it was still perfectly feasible that the shooting was accidental and had nothing to do with the investigation.

'We were like brothers when we were kids,' he said. 'Me and Geoff were rarely apart. Fought each other's battles, that sort of thing.'

'How did you meet him?' asked Davy Morrison.

'At the primary school in Levton Bridge. We both loved wildlife. That's how we connected. Over the nature table in class.' The memory brought forth a smile from the inspector. 'We walked miles on these hills. Saturdays. Summer holidays. Our folks never really bothered where we were half the time and Geoff was a big egg collector so we knew where all the nests were.'

'Wasn't it illegal?' asked Morrison.

'Still is, Davy, but Geoff was obsessed. He had hundreds of the things, kept them in a chest of drawers in his bedroom. Sold them for beer money from time to time. Besides, egg collecting was the least of our trouble with the law. That's why we drifted apart.'

'What happened?' asked Gallagher. He had heard the stories about the way the teenaged Jack Harris had left the valley after falling foul of the police but the inspector rarely talked about those days and many of the details were still shrouded in mystery.

'We fell into bad company,' said Harris. His expression seemed darker, more troubled, more distant, as the reflection from the flickering fire played across his face. 'We *were* bad company. It started when we transferred to the comprehensive school in Roxham. Nothing heavy to start with. Petty crime, poaching, vandalism, drunken disturbances in the park, that sort of thing. But I could see the way it was going. It came to a head when we left school. Me and Geoff had some terrible rows when I told him I wanted out. He accused me of betraying him and the other lads.'

'Is that why you left to go into the Army?' asked Gallagher.

'It was the only way I could see of keeping out of trouble. If I'd stayed, I'd have landed myself in prison, that's for sure. The local cops had got my card well and truly marked.'

'And Geoff?' asked Morrison. He looked at the body. 'What happened to him?'

'He came to the same conclusion as me. Just took a little longer. He went to prison for a couple of burglaries committed with one of the other lads. From what I heard, it was a real shock for him and, when he came out, he went down to Manchester to live with an aunt. Get away from the bad influences, steer clear of trouble.'

'And *did* he?' asked Morrison. 'Did he go straight?'

'As far as I know,' said Harris. 'Some of the others stuck with crime but not Geoff. He bought a lorry and started his own haulage business. It's done really well. I see loads of the trucks when I go down to see Jenny. Big green things with a couple of arrows down the side.'

'Not Speedwagonz, by any chance?' asked Morrison.

'Yeah, that's them.'

'I know Speedwagonz alright,' said Morrison. 'Sorry, sir, I know he was a friend, but I'm not sure that he *did* keep out of trouble. Well, not entirely anyway.'

'What makes you say that?' said Harris sharply.

Morrison hesitated before speaking further and Gallagher frowned – that sense of things unsaid again. The feeling that his boss was holding something back. Harris softened his tone.

'Sorry,' he said. 'Say what you have to say, Davy. I won't be offended. What do you know?'

'Well, before I came up here, I was with Lancashire Police and spent some time with Traffic, most of it on the M6. We had all sorts of bother with Speedwagonz.'

'What kind of bother?' asked Harris.

'Their drivers were always pushing it, skimping on the tachograph, cutting up their rivals, that sort of thing. They had loads of warnings and there were a couple of prosecutions. It's a competitive business, is haulage.'

'I guess it is,' said Harris.

Gallagher stayed silent; was he imagining it or had Harris looked relieved when Morrison mentioned traffic violations? As if he was expecting him to talk about something else? The sergeant shook his head slightly; he was probably imagining it. The darkness and the isolation playing tricks with his city-dweller's mind. And yet… and yet…

'But, like you say,' added Morrison, 'successful business. What brought Geoff back here?'

'The valley brings us all back eventually,' said Harris. 'She's like that. He bought a field on the edge of Levton Bridge and he's building his own home for when he retires. He's been living in a rented house in Levton Bridge so that he can oversee the build.'

'Yeah, I heard about that,' said Gallagher. 'It sounds very fancy, turrets, indoor swimming pool, games room, and all sorts. I bet Kevin McCloud would be interested.'

Morrison chuckled but Harris looked blankly at Gallagher.

'*Grand Designs*?' said the sergeant.

Still, Harris looked nonplussed.

'You really must buy a television, guv,' said Gallagher. 'So, was it like the old days when Geoff came back up here? Did you put your differences behind you? You've been seeing quite a bit of him, I think?'

'Yes, we have,' said Harris. 'And we were getting there. Bit awkward the first couple of times but it was getting easier. We had a lot of shared history. It counts for a lot, Matty lad.'

'It was like that with my best mate from the Met,' said Gallagher. 'I hadn't seen him for the best part of ten years then I bumped into him at a leaving do the last time I was in London. It was like we'd never been apart.'

'I did wonder if it was awkward between me and Geoff because of the bird club,' said Harris. 'He's always been big mates with Pete Guthrie and he knew that I was not happy with all the talk about direct action. We were due to watch the nest together tonight – I was down to replace Harry – and I had hoped that it might give us an opportunity to talk further.'

The inspector looked back towards the body.

'Somehow, I don't think that's going to happen now,' he said.

Chapter nine

The first pale streaks in the eastern sky heralded the arrival of dawn over the moor. As the light steadily strengthened, Harris looked down the slope towards the nest and breathed a sigh of relief. The inspector had taken the last watch of the night and, as the hours had passed, had become increasingly worried that daylight would reveal that the previous evening's disturbance had driven the hen harriers away.

Although Harris was relieved to see that the birds were still there, he feared that the coming morning's activity would see them finally abandon the nest. There was some hope, he thought as he watched them through his binoculars. He sensed that the young birds might be ready to fledge. Although he knew that such an event would normally be the time of greatest danger as they dispersed across the hills, making them more difficult to monitor, he hoped that no one would dare take another shot at them with a strong police presence on the moor. Assuming that was what lay behind the killing of Geoff Morden. And Jack Harris was entertaining serious doubts.

The distant rumble of engines cut into his thoughts and the inspector scanned the lower slopes of the moor with his binoculars. He struggled at first to see anything in the pale glow of dawn but was eventually able to make out pale pinpricks of light belonging to a couple of quad bikes making their way over the uneven ground. At the same time, the inspector heard the faint throb of a rotor blade behind him to the east and swung round to pick out the police helicopter which had just emerged over the far hills.

Harris looked at the dogs, who were watching him expectantly.

'You won't be able to move for people up here soon,' he said. 'It'll be like Piccadilly Circus.'

* * *

George Matthews did not sleep much as he lay in bed in the safe house, a semi-detached property in one of the more pleasant Manchester suburbs. Every time he found himself drifting into slumber, a sound in the darkness wrenched him back into consciousness. A creaking of timbers, a half-heard voice in the street, the slamming of a car door, all set his heart pounding with terror the likes of which he had never experienced. Now, with dawn having started to flood the bedroom with light, Matthews stared up at the ceiling and gave into the fears crowding in on him. He felt the tears welling up but wiped them away as there was a knock on the door and Gerry Bayliss walked in bearing a mug of tea.

'Figured you wouldn't be asleep,' said the detective sergeant. He noticed the streaks of tears on Matthews' cheeks and placed the drink on the bedside table. 'That might make you feel better, old son. I've put two sugars in.'

Matthews sat up in bed.

'Thanks,' he said. 'But I don't take sugar.'

'Then might I suggest you start?' said Bayliss. 'You're going to need all the energy you can get today. *Did* you sleep?'

'How could I?' said Matthews. He took a sip of the tea and grimaced at the sweetness.

'No, I didn't either.' Bayliss walked over to the window, pulled one of the curtains back slightly and peered down into the street, relieved to see that nothing was moving. 'You're going to have to get used to it. Not being able to sleep is an occupational hazard, I am afraid. Not sure I've had a proper night's sleep since I got the job with this bunch.'

'So, why do you do it?'

'Someone has to keep innocent members of the public safe from the criminal fraternity.' Bayliss turned back into the room and gave him a sly smile. 'Temptation, George, it's a terrible thing, eh? You, of all people, should know that.'

Matthews shook his head.

'I don't know what came over me,' he said.

'Greed,' said Bayliss. He peered through the curtain again and watched thoughtfully as a black car appeared at the end of the road. 'That's what came over you, old son. You aren't the first and you won't be the last. That's why they all do it.'

'So, what happens to me now?'

'You'll be moved in a couple of hours.' Bayliss watched as the black car cruised past the house, revealing two occupants. His lips moved as he memorised the registration plate before the vehicle disappeared from view. 'We'll go when the armed escort gets here.'

'Armed escort?' Matthews looked alarmed. 'Is that necessary?'

'You're in the big league now, George.'

As Matthews considered the comment, what little colour there was in his cheeks drained away.

'And where am I being taken?' he asked.

Bayliss did not answer immediately but instead took a notebook out of his back pocket and jotted down the registration number of the black car, resolving to check it the moment he had left the room.

'You'll be taken to one of our police stations,' he said as he completed his note. 'That's where you'll meet DCI Rutherford and the others.'

'What others?'

'The governor wants you to meet a couple of officers before he decides what to do next,' said Bayliss. 'You come with an awful lot of complications, you do, George.'

'And you're sure that no one knows where I am?' asked Matthews anxiously. 'I mean, can you keep me safe?'

'I learned a long time ago that you don't make promises in this game.' Bayliss looked through the gap in the curtains again and was relieved to see that the car had not returned. 'You might as well know it, Lynton Jago had a car parked near your house last night. We had to park a patrol car outside it in the end to scare them off.'

'But Esther's safe?' said Matthews.

'Yes. She's being held at another safe house.'

'How is she?'

'She's a mixture of frightened, worried and wanting to rip your head off and shit down the hole.'

'You really do need a better bedside manner,' said Matthews.

Bayliss smiled at the joke.

'You're going to need that sense of humour,' he said. 'It's no fun being on the wrong side of Lynton Jago.'

'Has his plane landed yet?'

'Haven't heard anything.' Bayliss glanced at his watch. 'Five to six. Any minute now. He's had people at the airport all night. We've had people there to keep an eye on them.'

'Are they going to arrest Jago?' asked Matthews hopefully.

'We're a long way off that, old son. A long way. When you lift someone like Lynton Jago, you have to be a hundred per cent sure. Could be days, could be months, could be never. The DCI has been trying for the best part of ten years.'

Matthews groaned.

'This is a nightmare,' he said. His voice was barely audible. 'Why did I do it? Tell me that, Gerry? Why did I steal his money?'

'Because you're like the rest of us.' Bayliss sat on the end of the bed. 'I often wonder if any of us would be able to turn down the chance to set ourselves up for life, if the opportunity presented itself.'

'Would *you* take it?' asked Matthews. 'Would *you* steal the money if you had the chance?'

'Not if it belonged to Lynton Jago, I wouldn't.' The sergeant stood up. 'Come on, finish your tea, get showered and I'll fix you some breakfast. You've got a big day ahead of you.'

The sergeant left the room and went into an adjoining bedroom where he booted up his laptop and tapped several times on the keyboard. It took the machine only a few seconds to come up with the list of vehicles and, when it did so, Bayliss opened his notebook and ran his finger down the numbers on screen, seeking a match with the one he had jotted down. He halted halfway through the list, glanced at his watch, and wondered if it was too early to ring Rutherford.

Chapter ten

As the police helicopter swooped across the moor, Harris reached into his haversack, produced a tin and a can opener and began to scoop the contents into a couple of bowls, watched eagerly by his dogs. He watched them eat for a few moments, turned his attention to coaxing fresh life into the fire and began to brew three mugs of tea, using water from one of the bottles propped up against a nearby rock.

Task done, he removed his smartphone from his coat pocket, walked down the slope so that he could not be heard and dialled 'P' from his contact list.

'Hello,' said a sleepy voice.

'It's Jack. You alone?'

'None of your business,' she said. 'Do you know what time it is?'

'Yeah, sorry about that, but it's been difficult to ring without anyone hearing.'

'Where are you?'

'Still on the moor. Guarding Geoff Morden's body.' Harris glanced back towards the tent and noted signs of movement. 'Look, I'm going to have to make this quick. I think this may have been a professional hit.'

'I thought you said it was an accident.' Her voice was alert. Sharp.

'Well, I was wrong.'

'That fucks things up. You haven't told anyone about what we've been doing, I hope?'

'Not yet, but if it *does* turn out to be deliberate, I'll have no option. They'll need to know. I mean, I can hardly argue that it's not relevant, can I?'

'*If* it's a hit, Jack. Have you told anyone about your suspicions?' she asked.

'Not yet.' Harris glanced over to the far side of the moor where the quad bikes were making good progress. 'But it won't be long before they work it out.'

'Ring me when you know for sure. I don't want to risk blowing everything by jumping to the wrong conclusion.'

'Yes, but–'

'Look, Jack, you know the rules.' Her voice had a harder edge now. 'I made them clear right from the start. We only take others into our confidence unless we really need to.'

'And in the meantime? What do I do in the meantime? I mean, I'll be leading a murder inquiry, for God's sake.'

'Like I said, just act normally.'

Harris was about to remonstrate with her when he noticed that Gallagher had emerged from the tent, bleary-eyed and yawning.

'Got to go,' said Harris and ended the call.

He walked back towards the tent just as Davy Morrison appeared through the flap, rubbing his shoulder to alleviate the discomfort of several hours lying on the rough ground. Gallagher noticed Harris slipping the smartphone back into his pocket.

'Anything interesting?' he asked.

'No, just checking with Control. Asking about the roadblocks.'

'Anything?'

'No.'

'He's away by now, isn't he?' said Morrison. He rubbed his aching shoulder again. 'I mean, there's no way he's going to try again with us here, is there?'

'I imagine not,' said Harris.

Gallagher looked across the moor.

'Are you sure that there's not a McDonald's?' he asked. He looked at the dog bowls, which had long since been licked clean. 'I'm not sure I fancy any of what they had.'

'Sorry, Matty lad,' said Harris. His phone rang and he fished the device out of his coat pocket. The inspector pointed to his bag. 'There's some emergency rations in there, if you want them. May fill a hole.'

He took the call.

'Gillian,' he said. 'Any updates?'

'One or two.' She sounded weary, the legacy of a night without sleep. 'I heard back from NPAS again and they've managed to rustle up another chopper. It should be with you soon and Doc and a ballistics guy are on their way up on quad bikes.'

'Yeah, I see them,' said Harris. 'I take it you've heard nothing from the roadblocks?'

'They've been stopping vehicles all night but come up with nothing, except a few locals. Oh, and you'll not be surprised to hear that we've been getting calls from the media. Someone tipped off local radio that something has happened. The press office is dealing with it.'

'Yeah, well, tell them that I don't want the media turning up here and trampling the nest site, will you?' said Harris. 'If they cut up funny, remind them that it's private land and they could get themselves arrested.'

'Will do.'

Harris slipped the phone back into his coat pocket.

'I thought you had already checked the roadblocks,' said Gallagher.

'Yes, but only with Control,' replied Harris. 'That was Gillian.'

'Right.'

Harris ignored the sergeant's unconvinced expression and returned his attention to making the tea. The three officers were halfway through their drinks and chocolate bars when the first of the quad bikes arrived, driven by a forensics officer. The second vehicle appeared at the bottom of the slope a couple of minutes later, steered by what they assumed to be an estate worker and bearing a white-haired man, who winced with pain as the machine clipped a large stone and momentarily went onto two wheels before coming to a halt close to the tent.

The Home Office pathologist got off the vehicle with some difficulty, grimaced again as he took a couple of moments to straighten his leg, picked up his walking stick and hobbled over to the officers.

'Couldn't you find somewhere more convenient, Hawk?' he grumbled. 'This has not exactly helped my arthritis.'

'And good morning to you, Doc,' said Harris. 'Sorry, but I wanted you to see the body in situ. I need to work out if this is accidental.'

'Or deliberate,' said Gallagher.

'Life would be much simpler if it was an accident,' said Harris.

'Yes, but–' began the sergeant.

'Why don't you let us work it out?' said Doc. He glanced at the ballistics investigator. 'Best not to get ahead of ourselves, eh?'

Neither Harris nor Gallagher replied. Within half an hour, the pathologist had completed his initial examination of the corpse and the ballistics officer had located the bullet which had missed the nest and embedded itself into the spongy ground. The two men returned to the tent.

'Accident?' said the inspector.

'Doubt it,' said the ballistics investigator. He held up the bullet, which was now in a plastic evidence bag. 'The first shot would certainly appear to have been aimed at the nest. It was only wide by three or four feet but the second one hit your guy in the heart. Stopped him in his tracks, didn't it, Doc?'

'He had absolutely no chance,' said the pathologist. 'He'd have died instantly.'

'Where did he fire from?' asked Harris.

The forensics investigator pointed to the slope leading up from the far side of the dip.

'Halfway up,' he said. 'There's a load of scuff marks where he crawled through the grass on his belly. I reckon he was lying down when he fired.'

'What kind of gun did he have?' asked Gallagher.

'A rifle. I'll know more when I get the bullet back to the lab.' The forensics officer glanced across to the far slope. 'If I was going to shoot at the birds, that's exactly where I would have positioned myself, but the second shot was as clean as they come. It feels like a kill shot.'

'I agree,' said Davy Morrison. It was the first contribution the firearms officer had made to the discussion. 'I thought that last night but, now that I've seen it in daylight, I'm even more convinced. Looks like a pro to me.'

'So, who knew that he was up here?' asked Gallagher. He looked at Harris.

'Everyone in the bird club had a copy of the rota for guarding the nest,' said the inspector. 'As did the estate office.'

'Why did they have a copy?' asked Gallagher.

'So, they knew who was on their land.' Harris looked at the ballistics investigator. 'Are you sure that it couldn't be an accident? I mean, can you rule it out completely?'

'Well…'

'You heard what he said,' protested Gallagher. 'You heard what all three of them said. They couldn't have been much clearer. Someone shot Geoff Morden deliberately. Maybe he was the target, not the birds.'

Harris did not have time to reply because his phone rang again.

'Gillian,' he said. He put the call on speaker so that the others could hear. 'Any developments?'

'Bob Crowther has just been on,' said Roberts. 'The mountain rescue team are ready to collect the body. Can they come up to you?'

Harris glanced at the ballistics officer and the pathologist, both of whom nodded. Half an hour later, six figures clad in red approached the tent. Team leader Crowther walked up to Harris.

'Someone said that it was Geoff Morden,' he said. He placed a hand on his old friend's shoulder. 'You OK?'

'I'll be fine, Bob.'

'We alright to take him?'

Harris looked at Doc.

'Yeah, that's fine,' said the pathologist. 'I'll have to do the post-mortem, of course, but it's pretty clear what killed him.'

'OK, guys,' said Crowther. He gestured to his team. 'Let's get him out of here. I'm sure the birds would appreciate some peace and quiet.'

Harris nodded his appreciation at the comment and the mountain rescue team loaded the body onto the stretcher. They were preparing to leave when two figures on foot appeared on the far side of the moor. Gallagher saw them first and tensed.

'We expecting guests?' he asked.

'I suspect it's the bird club guys.' Harris lifted his binoculars to his eyes. 'Yeah, it's the morning shift come to watch the birds. One of them is Pete Guthrie. Don't know the other chap that well. He doesn't come to many of the meetings. He's one of Pete's pals.'

'You want me to stay up here with them?' asked Morrison. 'Just in case the gunman is still around?'

'No, I'm pretty sure that he's gone.' Harris glanced across to where the helicopter had widened its search, swooping long and low in wide arcs over the moor. 'They'd have picked him up by now, if he hadn't. There's precious few hiding places. No, Bob's right, the sooner we all get out of here, the more likely it is that the birds will settle.'

* * *

It took the bird club members twenty minutes to arrive at the tent, passing the mountain rescue team on their way. Guthrie paused to look down at the dead man on the stretcher then quickened his pace and arrived at the tent almost at a run.

'Have you seen enough?' he said angrily. He jabbed a finger at Harris. 'You'd better get Masterson for this – and don't bleat on to me about proof! What more proof do you need? It's obvious that it's one of his men who killed him.'

'There's nothing obvious to say that is the case,' said Harris calmly.

'Who else could it be?' Guthrie glared at him. 'I told you that Masterson would try to get at the birds. Surely, you are not still protecting him?'

'I'm doing nothing of the–'

'Your friend is dead. Don't you care?'

Harris grabbed Guthrie by the front of his coat, lifting him up so that he was struggling to keep his feet on the ground.

'Of course, I fucking care!' rasped the inspector. 'How dare you suggest that I don't.'

Guthrie looked terrified and Gallagher stepped forward to intervene but Harris let the man go, the explosion of fury quelled as quickly as it had blown up.

'I'm sorry, Pete,' he said. 'That was uncalled for.'

Guthrie looked shaken, and relieved that the threat had passed. 'We're all upset.' He hesitated for a few moments, summoning the courage to pursue his point. 'I apologise for my comment, it was thoughtless, but I still say that it was one of Masterson's men. That's why we're going to continue watching the nest.'

'I'd rather you didn't.' The inspector noted that Gallagher was looking at him with an expression of growing consternation on his face and resolved to do what he could to quell the sergeant's suspicions. *Just act as you would normally.* 'I don't want to risk any more lives until I understand what has happened here.'

'Isn't it obvious?' said Guthrie. 'Someone went for the birds and hit Geoff.'

'We can't rule out that he was the target.'

'Who on earth would do a thing like that? No, it's one of Masterson's men, alright, and, if the police aren't going to take action, then somebody else needs to do something about it.'

'I told you last night, the last thing we want is anyone taking the law into their own hands. This is a time for calm heads.' Harris seemed unaware of the irony of the comment. 'Just leave it to us, will you?'

'OK, but we're staying,' said Guthrie.

Harris looked at his defiant expression.

'OK,' he said. 'But be careful. Whoever it is will probably be long gone but we can't be sure.'

* * *

The gunman *was* long gone. Following the shooting, he had made good progress across the moor and his pace had picked up dramatically with the advent of first light and the knowledge that he was approaching his car. His only moment of alarm came when the police helicopter approached from the east. He heard it before it emerged through the strengthening light of day and, as it neared him, the gunman took refuge in a wooded ravine. He shrunk down behind a rock, looking nervously skywards lest he be spotted by the crew who were scouring the expanse of moorland.

As the aircraft passed overhead, the scare injected fresh energy into the gunman's legs, a reminder that the job was not completed yet. Satisfied that the officers had not detected him, he watched until the aircraft was but a speck in the distance then turned and rapidly completed the last mile of his journey to a roadside copse. Having hidden in among the trees for a couple of minutes to assure himself that the police were not lying in wait – careful, always careful – the gunman gave a nod of satisfaction and walked towards the trees, where he unlocked the car and stowed the rifle in the boot. A minute later, he was driving along the narrow C-road, part of a network of minor routes that he was confident would allow him to avoid any police roadblocks.

An hour and a half later, and breathing more easily with every passing mile, he had found his way onto the southbound A1, north of Newcastle and his vehicle had blended into the rush-hour traffic. His job was done.

Chapter eleven

'Are you OK?' asked Gallagher, looking at Harris.

The inspector did not reply, concentrating instead on guiding the Land Rover along the rough track which led away from the moor and down to the main valley road. He had not spoken since they had climbed back into the vehicle and it felt to the sergeant like it was going to be one of his brooding silences.

'It's just that you haven't been quite yourself since the shooting,' said Gallagher. He was never one to be deterred by silence. 'And I know how difficult this must be for you. There's no shame in it, if you want someone else to take the lead, you know. I'm sure the DI would…'

'I wish people would stop telling me that I'm not up to the job,' said Harris.

'It's not that. It's just that it can be difficult when it's personal. When I was in the Met–'

'Not another of your fucking Met stories!' exclaimed Harris. He instantly regretted it. 'Sorry, Matty lad. You didn't deserve that.'

'I'm just concerned.'

'Yeah, I know you are and don't think that I don't appreciate your concern.'

'I mean, that blow-up with Pete back there…'

'I wondered when you'd bring that up,' said Harris.

'I can hardly ignore it. I've not seen you lose your temper like that for a long time.'

'Well, he was pushing it, wasn't he?' said Harris. He glanced across at the sergeant, who had grasped the seat as Harris drove across a bumpy stretch of track, without recourse to the brakes as usual – the vehicle rocking and rolling and the dogs thrown about in the back. 'Well, wasn't he?'

'I suppose so.'

Harris noticed that the sergeant still looked unconvinced.

'Look,' said the inspector, trying to sound conciliatory, 'I know that you and Gillian are worried about me, but I'll be fine. I shouldn't have lost my temper back there, I know that. It was out of order.'

'But what if Pete makes a formal complaint? After all, he's been hassling you ever since this birds thing started, hasn't he? I can't see him throwing up a chance like this to make trouble. Can you?'

'He won't complain,' said Harris. 'He likes people who are upfront about things, does Pete. It's the only way to handle him.'

'Does that include lifting him off his feet by the throat?'

'Probably not,' said Harris with a wry smile. 'Don't worry. It won't happen again.'

'And are you really happy to leave them up there guarding the nest when we don't know where the gunman is?'

'You know Pete Guthrie, Matty lad. Do you think he'd have agreed to anything else?'

'No, but…'

'They'll be fine. Whoever shot Geoff is well out of it.'

There was a sense of finality about the inspector's comment and Gallagher decided not to press the point;

he'd expressed his opinion like a good sergeant should do. Not that he was convinced that Harris had taken much notice; when Harris was in the mood, he was as bull-headed a man as the sergeant had ever encountered.

An uneasy silence settled on the vehicle and, five minutes later and with neither man having spoken, they rejoined the valley road. They followed it for a couple of miles before turning off and making their way along the tree-lined drive leading to Hewby Moor Estate, the Land Rover's tyres crunching on the gravel. A large white house appeared through the trees, all gable ends and ivy.

'Nice gaff,' said Gallagher. He tried to sound casual. Relaxed, as if the disagreement between the two men had not taken place.

'Old money,' replied Harris. 'The middle section dates back to the 1740s.'

'Always in the Masterson family?'

'I believe so.'

'But old money only goes so far, surely? It must be expensive to keep it all going.'

'It is, yes.' Harris pointed to the row of recently constructed stables in the yard not far from the house. 'But Henry Masterson is as modern as they come when it comes to money. They opened the equestrian centre last year, it's run by his wife, and they have a couple of fishing lakes which bring in a nice amount.'

'And then there's the grouse,' said Gallagher. 'Are they a good earner?'

'Are they ever. Folks come from all over to shoot on Henry's land.'

The irony of the comment was not lost on either man.

'Like who?' asked Gallagher.

'Everyone from businessmen who work in the City to shooting parties from abroad. I heard that Henry had a couple of groups come over from France last year. And one from Japan. Organised by a bloke at Nissan over

Sunderland way. Henry put them all up in The Hillview. Like it or not, grouse brings in a lot of money to this area.'

'And where there's money, there's a motive to stop anyone who gets in the way,' said Gallagher. 'And there is a dark side to it, isn't there?'

'Meaning?'

'Well, I used to know a guy who was into shooting. When I was working for the…' Gallagher's voice tailed off.

'It's alright,' said Harris. He gave the slightest of smiles. 'You can mention the Met.'

'I was just going to say that this guy was a local villain and him and a few of his mates used to travel up to Yorkshire for the Glorious Twelfth every year. Right rogues gallery, it was.'

'There were rumours of something similar last year,' said Harris. 'But that's all they were. I heard that one of the gang leaders from Merseyside organised a shooting party but when I asked Henry about it, he laughed it off. Said I shouldn't listen to local gossip.'

'Gossip or not, if it's such a lucrative business, he would have good cause to prevent the harriers leaving the nest, wouldn't he? Is Pete Guthrie right? Would Masterson be prepared to go as far as sending someone up with a gun? I mean, if he's got connections with gangland figures…'

'I think that may be putting it a bit strong,' said Harris. 'It's just business to him. Another booking. Money in the bank. Besides, he'd be a fool if he tried anything at a guarded nest, wouldn't he?'

'Maybe he had no option.' Gallagher was warming to his theme. 'Maybe the bad lads booked again. I wouldn't want to be the one to tell a bunch of villains that their fun weekend in the country is off because of a couple of overgrown spuggies. What if we were right all along, that Geoff *did* get in the way? It's like you always say, rule out the obvious before you try to complicate things – and who else would have reason to harm Geoff Morden?'

Gallagher waited for the inspector to offer his opinions on the theory but Harris lapsed back into silence instead. The sergeant did not have the chance to press the point further because, a couple of minutes later, the Land Rover pulled into the yard where the inspector brought the vehicle to a halt outside the stables, parking at the end of a row of mud-spattered quad bikes. The detectives got out and, as the inspector released his dogs, a tall, smartly dressed, grey-haired man wearing a flat cap and a Barbour jacket turned away from a conversation he was having with two estate workers and walked over. He reached down to pat Scoot and Archie.

'Hello, boys,' said Henry Masterson, ruffling their heads. The estate owner turned his attention to the inspector. 'I'm glad you've come, Jack. We need to get this sorted out.'

'We certainly do,' said Harris. He nodded towards his colleague. 'This is DS Matthew Gallagher. Not sure you've met.'

'No, we haven't. You are most welcome, Sergeant,' said Masterson. He surveyed their crumpled clothes and unshaven appearance. 'I take it you spent all night up there?'

'We did, yes,' said Harris.

'It's a nasty business alright. I hope that the two of you can clear things up pretty quickly.' Masterson's welcoming tone had been replaced by something harder-edged. 'I am not appreciating some of the insinuations that are being made. The actions of your officers last night left me very concerned. Very concerned indeed. Particularly Alison's behaviour.'

'That's Detective Constable Butterfield,' said Harris. 'This is an official police investigation, Henry.'

'Yes, well, you need to have a firm word with her.'

'About what?'

'She was asking a lot of questions about my staff. Demanding to see evidence that my gamekeepers were not out last night. Checking our gun cabinets and wanting to see our firearms certificates.' Masterson scowled. 'Like she thought that we could somehow have been involved in what happened. It's not on. Not on, at all.'

'She was only doing her job, Henry. And there *has* been a shooting on your land, remember.'

'Yes, but surely you do not believe that we could have anything to do with that?'

'Let's be honest, Henry,' said Harris. *Just act as you would normally.* 'You've not exactly been a fan of hen harriers down the years, have you?'

'And there's a lot of money at stake if the chicks fledge,' said Gallagher. 'I mean, an awful lot.'

'You're not from round here, are you?' said Masterson.

'No, I'm not,' said Gallagher; he hated it when people said that, as if his urban background somehow detracted from his ability to do his job. 'But I know enough to realise that dead hen harriers could work to your benefit.'

Masterson turned to Harris.

'Do I have to put up with this rubbish, Jack?' he protested. 'Or do I have to call you by your rank as well?'

'Until you and your people are ruled out of our investigation, yes. And don't look at me like that. The sergeant is only doing his job, just like Alison was. And your guys have been destroying hen harrier nests for years, have they not?'

'You've been listening too much to that hothead Guthrie,' said Masterson. 'I take it you've heard that he had a go at my estate manager in The Hillview the other night? Bill Harding's wife and kids don't have to listen to that sort of thing. His seven-year-old was in tears.'

'Yes, I–'

'I've warned Guthrie numerous times to be careful with what he says. I've even threatened him with an injunction and, like I told you, I've taken legal advice about suing him for slander.' Masterson gave Harris a hard look. 'And you and I have had the same conversation on more than one occasion down the years. I sincerely hope that I don't have to take things further with you as well. *Chief Inspector*.'

'I trust that you're not threatening me, Henry?'

The two men stared at each other in angry silence for a few moments. Gallagher held his breath; he'd never seen anyone threaten Jack Harris without some form of retaliation and the altercation with Guthrie on the moor was still fresh in his mind. For the second time that morning, he prepared to intervene but Masterson knew about Harris's reputation as well and was the first to soften his stance.

'Look, I don't want to fall out over this,' he said in a more conciliatory tone of voice. 'I mean, how many years have we known each other?'

'Must be approaching thirty,' said Harris. Gallagher was relieved to see that the inspector had retained control over his temper.

'Easily. I knew you and Geoff when you were snot-nosed kids scrumping apples from my orchard. And I seem to remember some carp going missing from one of my lakes one summer.' Masterson winked at Gallagher; an attempt to defuse the situation. 'I had to give your boss a clip around the ear on more than one occasion when he was a teenager. Right tearaway, he was.'

'Really?' Despite his concerns, Gallagher found himself smiling. Jack Harris was a big man and it stretched the sergeant's imagination to think of anyone clipping him round the ear, teenager or not. 'Is this true, guv?'

Harris gave the sergeant a rueful look.

'I'm afraid so,' he said. 'The fish cooked up nice, mind.'

'So, let's not fight,' said Masterson. 'You lost a friend last night, I realise that, and I am very sorry, but there is no need for wild accusations about the people who work on this estate. That's not fair to them. They're good people.'

'Maybe they are, Henry, but we would be failing in our duty if we didn't ask these questions,' said Harris. 'And you *do* detest hen harriers, everyone knows that.'

'Yes, but if I had wanted the birds dead, I would have done it before now.' The estate owner gave a half-smile. 'And shooting amateur ornithologists? It would not be the most intelligent thing to do, would it now? It's out of season, for a start.'

Harris gave him a sharp look and Masterson held up his hands.

'Sorry,' he said. 'That was in poor taste. Uncalled for. Listen, Constable Butterfield checked my people's alibis last night and seemed satisfied enough but I am keen to co-operate with your inquiry, so you can talk to them yourself if you feel that it is necessary.'

'My detective inspector seems satisfied with what they told DC Butterfield last night,' said Harris. 'Besides, I imagine that they'll only tell us the same thing, eh, Sergeant?'

'Well, since we're here, it might be worth–'

'We can always come back if we need to do more checks,' said Harris, cutting across him.

The sergeant frowned but said nothing.

'You'll have as much co-operation as you need, if you do.' Masterson gestured towards the house. 'Cup of tea before you leave? You look like you could do with one. Mary could probably even rustle you up a bacon sandwich, if you fancied it.'

'No, thanks. We'd better get back to Levton Bridge.' The inspector glanced at Gallagher, who had perked up at the thought of a bacon sandwich. 'There's an awful lot to do, isn't that right, Matty lad?'

Gallagher nodded gloomily.

'I am afraid so,' he said. 'Tempting as the thought is.'

With a couple of clicks, Harris recalled his dogs from their exploration of the stables and the officers returned to the Land Rover. Harris was about to climb into the driver's seat when a thought struck him and he turned back to look at the estate owner.

'How is it looking for the Glorious Twelfth, Henry?' he asked.

'Fully booked,' said Masterson. 'Could be our best year yet, if the weather holds. Just have to hope that your hen harriers keep away from the guns.'

Harris nodded, the officers climbed back into the vehicle and the inspector guided the Land Rover out of the yard.

'Shouldn't we have double-checked the alibis?' asked Gallagher as Harris steered the vehicle back onto the gravel drive. 'I mean, just to be sure?'

'Gillian seems happy and I trust her judgement. Besides, Henry Masterson has always been pretty straight with me.'

'Except when it comes to killing the hen harriers that are eating his grouse.'

'He knows I'll get him one day,' said Harris.

'Perhaps this is it,' said Gallagher. 'Perhaps he's overstepped the line this time. Or maybe one of his staff did. This Bill Harding fellow, perhaps.'

'I don't think so.' Harris slowed the vehicle down to allow a couple of sheep to cross in front of it. 'Henry's right, it would be a remarkably stupid thing to do.'

'But people do stupid things, don't they? And, alibis or not, I would still like to know more about what happened when Guthrie threatened Harding at The Hillview Hotel. Maybe something Guthrie said touched a nerve.'

'What, and Bill went out and shot the nearest ornithologist he could find?' said Harris. 'He's as even-tempered a man as you could ever hope to find. I can't see him doing something like that.'

'So where else do we look?' Gallagher was trying to conceal his irritation at the inspector. 'Maybe it's to do with what Davy Morrison was telling us about Geoff's haulage company?'

'What makes you say that?' asked Harris. It seemed to the sergeant that there was the slightest hint of anxiety in the inspector's voice.

'Well, like he says, it's a competitive business.'

'Competitive is one thing but it's a big jump to murder.'

'Well, there's *something* we don't know,' said Gallagher. 'A missing piece of the jigsaw.'

'Now that we can agree on.'

Not for the first time that morning, Gallagher waited for Harris to elaborate on his comment but, yet again, the inspector did not reply and an uneasy silence settled on the vehicle once more. Gallagher could not escape the troubling notion that there were things that his boss was concealing from him. Feeling a stab of guilt at having even entertained such a disloyal thought, he decided to ease the tension as Harris guided the Land Rover back onto the valley road and turned in the direction of Levton Bridge. Gallagher gave Harris an impish look.

'Scrumping?' he said.

'What?'

'I know you said that you were into some heavy stuff when you were a nipper, but stealing apples? Jeez, no wonder you had to leave. If the local cops had found out about that…' Gallagher shook his head and gave a low whistle. 'Well, I'm just saying.'

'If you tell anyone…' said Harris. He gave the sergeant a stern look but behind it lurked a smile.

'Who, me?' said Gallagher. He assumed his best innocent expression. 'Now, would I do a thing like that?'

However, it was only a brief exchange and the two men completed the rest of the journey to Levton Bridge in silence.

Chapter twelve

It was shortly after 9:00am when the car driven by Gerry Bayliss, containing a fellow officer and an anxious George Matthews, prepared to leave the safe house for its journey to the headquarters of the Organised Crime Unit. It was accompanied by an unmarked vehicle containing two members of the firearms team. As they were about to start the journey, Bayliss glanced in his rear-view mirror and frowned as he spotted the black car from earlier that morning drive slowly round the corner and into the street. The database had confirmed that it belonged to one of Jago's men and the sergeant reached for his radio.

'We got company,' he said. 'Time to do your thing.'

The black car slotted in behind the convoy as the police vehicles began to move but, within seconds, two marked patrol vehicles emerged from either end of the road. The black car turned off into the nearest side street and did not reappear, and the convoy reached its destination without further incident. There were no signs to identify the non-descript two-storey gated office block on the edge of one of Manchester's industrial estates and, after being taken through reception, Matthews was held in a small office with shuttered windows and only a table lamp for illumination.

Sitting alone in the claustrophobic half-light, his fears crowded in again and, as the minutes lengthened, he was filled with an overwhelming urge to leave. To take his chances with Jago. After all, he told himself, the police had no right to hold him. He'd given them no documentary evidence relating to the theft of the million. He could go whenever he wished. Matthews stood up and opened the door only to be confronted by a burly man who stood with crossed arms and stared wordlessly back at him.

Matthews took one look at the unsmiling features and went back into the office where he continued to wait until the door opened and the burly man gestured for him to follow him into the corridor, still without uttering a word. Matthews was ushered into another, larger room, also with shuttered windows. Sitting at the table were Ged Rutherford, a blonde woman in a dark business suit, and a slim, dark-haired man in uniform. All were grim-faced.

'Sit down, George,' said Rutherford. He gestured to the chair. 'This is Detective Inspector Jenny Armannsson, the head of our fraud squad, and PC Graham Leckie, who is one of our intelligence officers. They will be assisting me on the inquiry.'

Matthews took a seat and nodded a welcome. Armannsson and Leckie gave the merest of nods in return as they surveyed him with interest. Very rarely were they presented with such opportunities when delving into the dark underbelly of organised crime and, on first impressions, the man returning their gaze out of haunted eyes did little to inspire confidence.

'Did you sleep well?' asked Rutherford. He did not sound like he cared. 'The accommodation up to your requirements? Although, having had to suffer Gerry's tea…'

He did not complete the sentence and a smile flickered across Leckie's face. Before Matthews could reply, Bayliss entered the room and placed a mug of tea in front of him.

'Ah, speak of the devil,' said Rutherford. 'The devil's brew, anyway.'

Matthews nodded his thanks at the sergeant and gratefully took a sip as Bayliss left the room. He noted that there was no sugar this time.

'I didn't sleep at all,' he said.

'I'm not surprised,' said Rutherford. 'Neither did I. Now then, DI Armannsson here has been examining the documents that you gave us last night, haven't you?'

'I have,' said Armannsson. She flicked through the large pile of papers on the desk. 'The trouble is, George, all they confirm is that Lynton Jago is a keen investor. There is nothing to suggest criminal behaviour. Nothing to say where the money came from.'

'It came from crime,' said Matthews.

'I am sure it did but we have to be able to establish the link, otherwise his lawyer will laugh us out of court.' Armannsson picked up the top few sheets of paper then dropped them back onto the pile. 'I'm not sure that any of these do that.'

'However,' said Rutherford, 'there is still a chance that you may be of assistance. You'll have heard of the Proceeds of Crime legislation, I assume?'

Matthews nodded.

'Lynton talked about it quite a bit,' he said.

'I'm sure he did,' said Rutherford. 'You may well know, then, that the legislation allows us to seize his assets if we can convince the court that he earned the money through crime. However, we've tried that with Jago a couple of times already and we failed on both occasions. He's got a particularly sharp lawyer so, although I'm not ruling out another attempt based on what you have given us, what we really want is something that allows us to lock him up. What else do you know, George?'

'I hear things.'

'I'm sure you do but we need something more than hearsay.' Rutherford glanced at the pile of documents. 'All this little lot does is prove that he's got a particular interest in emerging economies in Eastern Europe. As the DI said, it's hardly a crime, is it?'

Matthews did not reply but looked bleakly across the table at Rutherford.

'How come you were able to steal Jago's money in the first place?' asked Armannsson. 'I am assuming that he deals with you direct?'

'Every time,' said Matthews. 'If you ask me, I don't think that he trusts the others.'

'And why would he trust *you*?' asked Leckie. It was the first time he had spoken since Matthews had entered the room. 'With all due respect, you do not look like the type to be part of organised crime.'

'I think that's why he picked me.' Matthews gave a sad smile. 'Someone he could intimidate and who wouldn't ask too many questions. I'm ideal.'

'So, if you're Mister Perfect, how come that this time you took his money?' asked Leckie.

'Lynton made a mistake this time. See, he usually rings me the day after our meeting to check that I've invested the money and he demands documentary proof. He's very careful is Lynton.'

'But this time was different?' said Leckie.

'Yes. This time, he told me that his daughter was getting married in the Caribbean and that he would be away for a week. He said he trusted me and that he'd check when he got back. I don't know what came over me. I wasn't thinking straight.'

'You were thinking straight enough to put the money into an offshore account in the Canary Islands,' said Armannsson pointedly. She picked up the top sheet. 'And move it twice.'

Matthews said nothing.

'Have you talked to Jago since he discovered you had stolen the money?' asked Leckie.

'No, but he rang me three times yesterday from the Caribbean. I didn't dare ring back but I knew what he wanted. I knew that Esther would be at work so I went straight home, packed a bag and went to the airport.'

'Trouble is,' said Rutherford, 'they are the actions of a guilty man, are they not? Nick the money and hop on a plane.'

He looked at his colleagues. Leckie and Armannsson nodded.

'You see, as it stands, Mr Matthews,' continued Rutherford, 'the only person who has committed a crime that we can actually prove is you.'

Beads of sweat glistened on Matthews' forehead and Rutherford gave a slight smile; the tactic of keeping the financial advisor frightened was working beautifully. Long experience of gangland investigations had taught the DCI that it was crucial that informants were more frightened of the police than the villains. Given Lynton Jago's reputation, that meant playing it tough.

'Now, if you could think of anything else to help us ...' said Rutherford. He left the sentence hanging.

'Like what?' asked Matthews eagerly.

Rutherford glanced at Armannsson.

'Any ideas, Inspector?' he asked.

'Well, tracking illegally sourced money through major financial institutions is tricky,' she said. 'Takes a lot of time and effort. However, it would be easier if Jago was also investing in smaller concerns. That's much easier to prove. Was this the only money that Jago was laundering, George? Did it all go in stocks and shares?'

'No,' said Matthews. 'He invested in a few companies as well. I didn't deal with that, though, it's just what I heard.'

'Do you happen to know which companies?' asked Rutherford, leaning forward in his seat.

Matthews thought for a few moments.

'I think a couple of them were technology businesses in Salford,' he said. 'I don't know their names. One develops apps for the games industry, I think. Oh, and he was also putting money through the books of a haulage company in Manchester. It's got one of those funny names. It has a Z on the end.'

'Speedwagonz?' asked Leckie. 'I pass their depot on the way in to work.'

'Yes, that's them. Mr Jago mentioned the name of the man who runs it a couple of times.' Matthews furrowed his brow as he tried to dredge the memory up from the recesses of his mind. 'Morden. Yes, that's it. Geoff Morden.'

'Now that name rings a bell,' said Leckie. The constable reached down and extracted his laptop from his bag and placed the device on the table. He typed, waited for the information to come up then scrolled down the page. 'In fact, I am pretty sure that I read it this morning. Morden, Morden. Ah, yes, here it is. Geoff Morden. Got himself shot dead last night.'

The colour drained from Matthews' face.

'And how come I don't know about it?' asked Rutherford.

'Because it happened out of our area.' Leckie opened up a document and a smile flickered across his face. 'Ooh, you'll like this, sir. It happened near Levton Bridge.'

Rutherford gave him a sharp look.

'Levton Bridge?' he said. 'Isn't that…?'

'It is indeed.'

'Wonderful,' said Rutherford. He closed his eyes and sighed. When he opened them again, he looked accusingly at Armannsson. 'Don't tell me that we're going to be working with your boyfriend on this one?'

'Don't blame me,' said Armannsson.

Leckie read from his laptop again.

'I'd say that it's pretty much definite,' he said. He was trying not to laugh at Rutherford's appalled expression. 'Jack Harris is the senior officer in the case. According to the report, the early theory is that Morden was shot accidentally while protecting a hen harrier nest.'

Rutherford looked blank.

'Birds,' said Leckie. 'They eat red grouse.'

Rutherford looked none the wiser.

'I'll explain later,' said Leckie with a smile. 'Suffice to say that if there's more to it than accidental shooting, and if there's a possible connection between the shooting and Lynton Jago, Jack Harris will sure as hell want to know about it. You know how pissed off he was that he never got to lift him when he was here.'

'Brilliant,' said Rutherford. Suddenly, he felt very tired. Maybe he should have taken that week's holiday when the opportunity had presented itself. It was not as if his wife hadn't nagged him about it. 'That's all I bloody need. Return of the fucking prodigal son.'

Leckie burst into laughter. Armannsson was not sure what to think and George Matthews simply looked bewildered.

'I don't understand,' he said to Leckie when the constable's mirth had subsided. 'Who is this Jack Harris fellow?'

'He's like us, George, but without the natural easy-going charm.' Leckie glanced at Armannsson, devilment in his eyes. 'Depending if he likes you or not, that is. I gather that he can be quite a pussycat when you get him in the right mood. Eh, Inspector?'

Armannsson looked embarrassed.

'But as for everyone else,' said Leckie, 'he's pretty much your worst nightmare. Isn't that right, Mr Rutherford?'

'Definitely,' said Rutherford. 'And I never saw the pussycat.'

* * *

The exchange did little to ease George Matthews' fears and the financial advisor would have found his anxiety levels heightened even further had he been able to witness the events taking place in an office just five miles from the police station. The room was behind the second-hand car showroom which afforded Lynton Jago the legitimate front for his illegal activities and it was a worried owner who sat behind the large oak desk.

A muscular, lean man in his mid-fifties, Jago was not his usual neatly turned-out self, following his overnight flight from the Caribbean. His clothes were crumpled, he was unshaven and there were dark bags underneath his eyes caused by his inability to sleep on the plane. Sitting in his featureless office with its bare walls, the happiness of his daughter's beach wedding seemed a long time ago and Jago had a throbbing headache. He stared balefully at the two men who were standing in front of him, watching their boss nervously.

'So,' he said, in a quiet voice that they both knew meant trouble. 'Do we know if the police have arrested Matthews or not? Will someone fucking well tell me?'

'They must have,' said the burly man with the scar running across his right cheek. 'They were at his house all night. We couldn't get close.'

'But did anyone actually see them take him away?' asked Jago.

'No, but we've had people looking everywhere and had people at the airport all night. No one has seen him. The police *must* have him. We're checking all their safe houses.'

'Well, if they do have him,' said Jago grimly, 'we must assume that they've got my money as well.'

'But are you sure that he's taken it?' asked the second man. Stuart Davis was slim and dressed in a dark suit but no tie. 'Surely, there's no way that he would dare to cross–'

'Yes, I'm sure!'

'But–'

'I'm not a bloody fool!' said Jago. The volume of his voice had risen.

'No, I wasn't saying that…' Davis looked alarmed and fell silent.

'You'd better not be.' Jago's voice was quiet again. Laden with menace. 'And, yes, I do think that he's stolen the fucking money. I'm just not quite sure how the police found out.'

'But there's no way he will talk,' said Scarface confidently. 'He knows what you'll do to him if he does.'

'But what if he's more frightened of Rutherford?' said Jago. 'Because if that's who has got him, they'll be piling the pressure on thick. You know what they're like.'

'Yeah, but what does he know?' asked Davis. 'George Matthews is a nothing.'

'He's a nothing who knows more than you think,' said Jago. 'And if Rutherford's mob *have* got him, we could have big problems…'

Chapter thirteen

It was just after 10:00am when Harris and Gallagher, both preoccupied with their own thoughts, returned to divisional police headquarters, which was housed in a Victorian building on the steep hill leading down from Levton Bridge marketplace. The inspector parked the Land Rover in front of the station – the divisional commander did not like officers doing it, so he always left it there – and the two men got out of the vehicle. Brusquely waving away questions from the gathered journalists, Harris led the way into the building. Gallagher paused at the top of the steps to exchange a few pleasantries with a couple of the reporters then followed his boss into the station.

Once inside, the inspector headed to his office without speaking and, after watching him go, Gallagher sighed and walked along the corridor to the detective inspector's office where he hesitated with his hand raised against the door. He thought about turning back then shook his head.

'I shouldn't be here,' he murmured and knocked.

'Come in,' said Gillian Roberts.

The sergeant entered to find her sitting at her desk, looking weary and heavy-eyed as she sifted through a pile of reports. She took in his dishevelled appearance and raised an eyebrow.

'By, you're really rocking the rustic look,' she said. '*Country Life* coming to do a photoshoot?'

Unusually, Gallagher did not smile at the joke.

'What's wrong?' asked Roberts; it was rare that the sergeant suffered a sense of humour failure.

'Everything's wrong,' said Gallagher. He closed the office door and sat down heavily opposite her. 'I'm probably about to end my career, for starters. Certainly, at Levton Bridge. And I want you to know that I've never done anything like this, ma'am. I'm not even sure that I should be here.'

'Well you are, so spit it out.'

'It's not like I'm not used to Jack's ways,' said the sergeant. 'He's not the easiest of men to work with.'

'Gettaway.'

Still, Gallagher did not smile but instead stared down at the desk for a couple of moments, appearing to take an intense interest in a knot in the wood. Roberts allowed him time to gather his thoughts and eventually he looked up again.

'What's troubling you, Matthew?' said Roberts softly. 'You clearly came here to say something.'

Gallagher sighed.

'Ever since Geoff Morden was shot, Jack has been acting strangely,' he said. 'And I'm concerned that it's jeopardising the investigation.'

'In what way is he acting strangely?' asked Roberts.

'Distracted. Unwilling to engage in conversations about the case. It's like he can't focus. One moment he's thinking one thing then the next it's something else.'

'That's not like him. In my experience, Jack Harris usually knows his own mind.'

'Exactly.' Gallagher looked relieved that he was able to talk about what had been troubling him. 'If you ask me, ma'am, he's torn between not wanting to think that his old friend Geoff Morden might have done something which warranted killing him but also not wishing to believe that Henry Masterson might be involved. They may disagree about birds of prey but it's obvious that there's a long-standing relationship between the two of them.'

'They certainly go a long way back,' said Roberts. 'And you reckon all of this is threatening the investigation, do you?'

'Yeah, I do. I reckon that the governor is far too close to this one and I am worried that we're losing opportunities. He wouldn't even agree to double-check the gamekeepers' alibis when we were up at the estate. I know that you were happy with them but it can't harm to check again, can it?'

'No, it can't.'

'Then there's what happened with Pete Guthrie up on the moor earlier this morning,' said Gallagher. 'I thought that Jack was going to hit him.'

'Really?' Roberts sat forward in her chair. 'What brought that on? Guthrie's big mouth, I imagine.'

'He suggested that the governor wasn't concerned about the death of his friend. Look, I hate doing this, ma'am, but if Guthrie makes a complaint and I didn't say anything…'

'No, you've done the right thing, Matty. Maybe Hawk *is* too close to this one. He does like to present a macho image to the world.' She gave him a reassuring smile. 'Leave it to me, I'll sort it.'

'Can you make sure he doesn't know that it's come from me?' said Gallagher.

'Jack Harris is one of the finest detectives I have ever worked with, Matty. How long do you think it'll take him to work it out?'

The sergeant nodded gloomily.

'Michaelmas daisies,' he said.

'What?'

'That's what I would like on my coffin.'

Roberts chuckled.

'Don't worry, I'll look after you, lovey,' she said.

'It's not you looking after me that I'm worried about,' said the sergeant.

* * *

Harris had been in his office for an hour, during which time he dozed fitfully as the exertions of the long night on the moor caught up with him. His slumber was disturbed by a knock on the door and a slim, balding uniformed officer walked into the office. Divisional Commander Philip Curtis frowned as he noticed the dogs lying next to the radiator. Although he and Harris had worked hard to develop a good working relationship after a fractious start to the commander's tenure, the presence of the animals at the police station remained a point of contention. However, Curtis knew that the animals were popular with the rest of the staff so, as usual, he opted to say nothing on the subject. Besides, he had more serious matters to discuss. Play this one wrong and he would destroy all the good work that had gone into establishing their relationship.

'How's it going?' asked Curtis as he sat down.

'It's been better.'

'So I hear. I've just come off the phone from Henry Masterson.' Curtis tried to sound casual. Relaxed. The last thing he wanted was an argument. 'He's not happy with you.'

'You checking up on me?' Harris looked suspiciously at the commander.

'Actually, *he* rang me.'

'Why?'

'He claims that you didn't take his complaint about DC Butterfield seriously. He's worried that your personal feelings are colouring the investigation.' Curtis adopted a softer tone. 'Look, I know that Geoff Morden was a friend and I can ask headquarters to send someone else up to lead the inquiry if you need to step back from this one. Or maybe Gillian can…'

'I'll be fine,' said Harris.

'Will you, though?'

'What does that mean?'

'I'm hearing things,' said the commander.

'What kind of things?' Harris shot him another suspicious look.

'That not only are you struggling with the death of a friend, but you're also unwilling to consider the possibility that Henry Masterson could be involved.'

'And where did you hear all this?' said Harris sharply. 'As if I didn't know?'

'Never mind where it came from, Jack, if you can't handle–'

'I told you, I'll be fine.'

'Then convince me,' said the commander. This time, his tone was clipped. Business-like. 'The chief's office has been on three times already this morning. Give me something to tell them. Let's start with the accidental death theory. Do you buy it?'

'It's looking unlikely.'

'So why would someone want to shoot Geoff Morden?'

Harris did not reply. The silence lengthened.

'You can see why people are worried, can't you?' said Curtis. 'If personal issues are getting in the way, it's not something I can ignore, Jack. I have to do something about it.'

As Harris tried to formulate his answer, he could feel the anger rising. Not at Curtis for challenging him, not at Gallagher for going over his head, but at himself. Jack Harris had built his career on a reputation for being in control of events and he hated giving the impression that this time they were controlling him. Every fibre in his body urged him to take the commander into his confidence. Tell him what was really happening. The secrecy had not been a problem when Geoff Morden was alive – no one at

Levton Bridge Police Station had taken more than a passing interest in the businessman and even when they did, it was usually about his new house – but now that he was dead, everything had changed. Harris saw the concerned look on the commander's face and resolved to stop playing the game by other people's rules. But before he confronted Susan Peters, he had to give Curtis reason not to remove him from the case. To buy himself some time.

'I'm sorry, sir,' said Harris. Maybe using the word 'sir' would help, he thought. 'A bit short on sleep, that's all, and it's true, I am upset about Geoff's death but, you're right, that should not get in the way of the inquiry. We'll be looking into every aspect of his life.'

'Like what?'

'His role in the arguments over the harriers, for starters, as well as anyone who might have born a grudge about the activities of his haulage company. Speedwagonz were not exactly popular. And we'll look into his private life as well. Maybe there's something there. His wife died several years ago and we'll try to find out if he had entered into a new relationship. I'd heard nothing but it's not exactly the kind of thing that we talked about.'

'It's a start,' said Curtis. Although still unconvinced about the inspector's commitment, the commander decided not to push the point. He stood up and headed for the door. 'Enough to be going on with, at any rate, but be warned, the chief will want to see progress. I'll pop back later.'

The commander left the room and his voice drifted back from the corridor.

'So long as you don't mind me checking up on you, that is,' he said.

Harris allowed himself a slight smile.

'Smart Alec,' he murmured. His expression darkened and he reached for his smartphone, which was lying on the desk. 'I'm sick of this. No one plays me for a fool.'

The inspector was unable to make the call, however, because his desk phone rang. He sighed and picked up the receiver.

'DCI Harris,' he said.

'Hiya, you,' said Jenny Armannsson.

'Now then. Hope you don't want a chat because I'm a bit busy.'

'That's why I'm ringing,' she said. 'It looks like your shooting may well be linked to something on which I have just been called in.'

Alarm bells started to ring for Harris. This was unravelling and unravelling rapidly.

'Oh?' said Harris. He tried to sound unconcerned. 'How come?'

'It seems that Speedwagonz have been doing a bit more than running a few lorryloads of tinned tomatoes up and down the M6.'

Harris closed his eyes. How on earth could she have found out? He and Susan had been careful to keep their investigation under the radar. The inspector sat with the phone dangling in his hand for a few moments as the ramifications played out in his mind.

'You still there?' asked Armannsson.

'Yeah, sorry. What have Speedwagonz been doing then?'

'Can we meet?' she said. 'The DCI says that he doesn't want to discuss it on the phone.'

'What DCI?' More alarm bells.

'Ged Rutherford.'

This was getting worse, thought Harris bleakly.

'How come Organised Crime are interested in Geoff?' he asked.

'I've already said too much.'

'Can't you tell me anything?'

'Not on the phone. And Ged doesn't want you to come down here, either. He wants to meet well out of our area so that we're not seen.' She lowered her voice. 'This is heavy stuff, Jack. I've never seen him so on edge.'

'Yes, well, I'll need a bloody good reason to persuade my commander that I should leave the area in the middle of a murder inquiry,' said Harris. 'He's already thinking of replacing me because I'm personally involved.'

'Let's just say that there could be a link between Geoff Morden and Lynton Jago.'

'OK, you've piqued my interest. Where do you want to meet?'

* * *

Phone call completed, Harris sat back in his chair, sipped at his mug of tea and let his thoughts roam. Mention of Lynton Jago had sparked memories of his days in Manchester, days in which he operated at the sharp end of the force's investigation into the city's crime gangs. Memories of surveillance operations, dawn raids and interviews in dimly lit rooms laden with fear and menace. And memories of the mocking smile of the man who got away. Of unfinished business. Of Lynton Jago.

Harris wrenched his thoughts back to the present day and reached for the smartphone again. He had just dialled the number for Susan Peters when there was a knock on the door. The inspector quickly replaced the phone on the desk and looked up to see Matty Gallagher enter the room.

'I can come back,' said the sergeant. He gestured to the phone.

'No, it's alright. What can I do for you, Matty lad?'

'Thought I'd pop up to The Hillview Hotel,' said Gallagher. He tried to conceal his relief that Harris did not seem to know about the conversation with Roberts. 'I know you're not convinced that Bill Harding might be involved but I'd still like to get to the bottom of the bust-up with Guthrie.'

'Good idea.'

'Really?'

'Yes, but send someone else.' Harris drained his mug, stood up and put on his jacket. 'And get your coat. You and I have something much more exciting to do.'

He strode out of the room, dogs at his heels.

'Like what?' Gallagher was startled – and delighted – by the return of the inspector's sense of purpose. Delight was quickly replaced by uneasiness; the sergeant was beginning to regret his talk with Roberts. Had he misread the situation? Misjudged his boss? He followed Harris out of the office. 'Where are we going?'

'I'll tell you on the way,' said Harris. He strode down the corridor, the sergeant struggling to keep up with him. 'Just need to get someone to look after the dogs. I'll see you in the car park in a quarter of an hour.'

'I thought you left the Land Rover out the front?'

'Yes, but we're going in yours,' said Harris. 'We don't want to get recognised.'

'Recognised by who?'

Before Harris could reply, his mobile rang. Harris stopped walking and took the call.

'Give me a minute,' he said into the device. The inspector gestured for Gallagher to continue walking. 'I'll see you at the car.'

When Gallagher had gone, Harris checked that no one else was in the corridor and returned his attention to the caller.

'Sorry about that, Susan,' he said.

'You rang but it cut off,' said Peters. 'What do you want?'

'I rang to say that it's time to stop playing games. I'm being made to look a fool and I don't like it.'

'I take it this is about Geoff?'

'It's looking pretty certain that he was murdered and we both have a good idea why. What's more, I have this nasty feeling that Ged Rutherford knows something about it as well. He's asked to see me.'

'Why should Organised Crime be interested in Geoff Morden?' Her voice betrayed alarm.

'They think that there may be some sort of link between Geoff Morden and Lynton Jago,' said Harris.

'Really?' said Peters. 'That's new. Could Jago be the middle-man in the UK?'

'It's a possibility. He'll do anything so long as it makes him money and he's certainly got the network to handle something like this. Maybe you, me and Ged are all investigating the same thing.'

There was silence on the other end as Peters considered the comment.

'Fuck,' she said eventually. 'Fuck, fuck, fuck.'

'Indeed, and it means that I have to tell my people,' said Harris. 'I have no option now. In fact, you could make a good case for charging me with obstructing a murder inquiry, if I don't.'

'I guess so,' she said. 'But only tell who you need to. When are you seeing Rutherford?'

'Half one.'

'I think I should be there. Where are you meeting him?'

Harris told her, ended the call and allowed himself a satisfied smile. He was back in control.

Five minutes later, he was sitting in Philip Curtis's office with the commander, Roberts and Gallagher looking at him expectantly. The transformation on the man of an hour previously was startling. His eyes gleamed and his body language told of pent-up energy and they were intrigued at what they were witnessing.

'I think I owe you an explanation,' said Harris. 'You see, there's something you need to know about Geoff Morden but I'm only telling you on the condition that it does not go out of this room. Not yet anyway.'

Chapter fourteen

It was mid-morning and Lynton Jago sat at his desk with his eyes closed as the weariness of his journey from the Caribbean caught up with him and he waited for the painkillers to reduce the throbbing sensation in his head. There was a knock on the office door and Jago opened his eyes and winced at the impact from the light.

'Come in,' he said.

Stuart Davis entered and gave a slight shiver. As ever, he was struck by the fact that, however warm the day, there was always a sharp chill in the air in Lynton Jago's office.

'Any news?' asked Jago.

'The radio's running the story about Geoff Morden now.'

'What did it say?'

'That the police think it was an accident,' said Davis. 'That he was shot while protecting the birds.'

'Good,' said Jago. 'Who's leading the investigation? Is it Jack Harris?'

'Yes.'

Jago scowled. As ever, mention of Harris sparked memories of the detective's days in Manchester. Jago remembered Harris's words the final time they had met before the detective left the city to take up his new post in Levton Bridge. 'I'll get you,' Harris had said through gritted teeth. 'So, help me, Lynton, one day I'll get you.' The words had stayed with Jago, a man who was not used to being threatened. Now, he shook his head to banish the memories and wished he hadn't, as a sharp stab of pain made him wince again.

'You OK?' asked Davis.

'No, I'm not fucking OK. You'd better be right. Harris had better not come down here asking questions. The last thing we want is him back in Manchester causing trouble again.'

'I don't think he will. He can't possibly know about our link with Speedwagonz.'

'Nevertheless, I don't like the idea of either him or Ged Rutherford poking their noses into the business.' Jago frowned. 'No, there's too much heat for my liking at the moment. We may have to lie low for a while. At least until it blows over.'

'But what about the shipment?' asked Davis. 'We're still OK for that, yeah?'

'Postpone it,' said Jago.

'But everything's ready. And we promised them that–'

'The revolution can wait.'

'But…'

'I said postpone it.' Jago's voice was harsh.

'Yes, of course,' said Davis quickly as he saw the darkening expression on his face. 'You're right, of course. Far too risky. What do I tell them?'

'Tell them to give it a couple of weeks to let things quieten down. It should be alright then.' Jago looked worried as a thought struck him. 'Unless, of course, George Matthews knows about Speedwagonz.'

'How can he?'

'He's a listener, that one.'

’m sure that he doesn’t know anything,’ said Davis.

‘But you don’t know that for certain, do you?’ said Jago. He looked increasingly anxious. ‘Who knows what the little toerag has picked up over the years? Do we know where he is yet?’

‘We’re guessing that the police took him to their station on the industrial estate.’

‘Guessing?’ said Jago suspiciously. ‘Don’t you know?’

Davis hesitated.

‘Not for certain,’ he said eventually.

‘Well, find out *for certain*. I don’t want any more fuck-ups. I want George Matthews silenced. Is that clear?’

‘Yes, but how can we do that?’ protested Davis. ‘Organised Crime have got him locked up tight.’

‘That,’ said Lynton Jago, closing his eyes again as another wave of pain overwhelmed him, ‘is your problem. Just make sure that it gets done.’

It seemed to Davis that the temperature had dropped another couple of degrees in the office.

Chapter fifteen

'So, when did MI5 get in touch with you?' asked Gallagher.

'Seven or eight weeks ago,' replied Harris. 'Once they knew that Geoff had moved back to Levton Bridge.'

The officers were in Gallagher's car as the sergeant drove through the flattening hills on the way to the southbound M6. A more cautious driver than his boss, particularly on winding rural roads that he did not know well, Gallagher was hardly touching 50mph and Harris kept glancing anxiously at the dashboard clock. Eventually, the sergeant looked across at him.

'We're meeting them on the third set of services down, aren't we?' he said.

'Yeah. At the little hotel on the back road.'

'We'll be OK for time then. We're not all Lewis Hamilton.' Gallagher was feeling more relaxed in the inspector's presence the longer that his meeting with Gillian Roberts went without being mentioned.

'Who?'

'Never mind. So, how long had they been tracking Geoff?'

'They'd known for a while that one of his drivers had been talking to the Kosovans,' said Harris. 'It seemed safe to assume that Geoff knew about it. He was very hands-on. Nothing came into that depot or left it without him knowing. When Susan Peters heard that he was moving to Levton Bridge, she rang me.'

'Why you? You don't have a connection with MI5, do you?'

'No, but she knew me from her days with the Greater Manchester Police. She was a DS before she went to join the spooks.'

'And exactly how well did she know you?' asked Gallagher.

'We attended a couple of courses together.'

'That's not what I was thinking.' Gallagher shot his boss a sly look.

'I know exactly what you were thinking.'

'Can you blame me?' said Gallagher. 'You *do* have something of a reputation when it comes to attractive police officers, do you not? I assume she's attractive?'

'She is, yes.'

'Blonde, I take it?'

'No.'

'But you still…?'

'As she is constantly reminding me, some things are on a need-to-know basis – and you don't need to know.' Harris gave the sergeant a sharp look. 'And neither does Jenny. This all happened seven years ago. Long before we met each other.'

'Point taken.' The sharpness of the comment had served as a timely reminder to the sergeant that he still needed to take care with Jack Harris. 'So, what exactly did she ask you to do?'

'She wondered if we could run some covert surveillance on Geoff. It was my idea for me to get close to him, see what I could find out.'

'Wasn't the fact that he knew that you were a copper a problem?'

'Susan certainly needed a lot of persuading but, like I told her, it would have looked strange if me and Geoff didn't meet up, given our long-standing friendship. The hen harriers were a godsend. They gave us a reason to talk. It was a case of hidden in plain sight. Besides, Geoff always believed that, deep down, I was still the same person who ran with the boys on the wrong side of the law all those years ago.'

'You certainly have your moments,' said Gallagher. He uttered the words almost without realising that he had done it and immediately regretted the comment.

Harris looked intently at him.

'I take it you were the one who told Curtis that I'd lost the plot?' he said. The voice was calm. 'That there was something off?'

'What makes you think that?' Gallagher tried to sound surprised and focused intensely on his driving, attempting to ignore the quickening of his pulse and the beads of sweat that had started up on his forehead. 'I haven't talked to Curtis today.'

'Well, someone did, and I think it was you.' There was an edge to the inspector's voice now. 'Next time you have a problem with me, you come to me, yeah? Don't take it to Curtis first.'

'I didn't.'

'OK, if you want to play silly buggers, don't take it to the DI then. It puts Gillian in a very difficult situation.'

Gallagher nodded glumly. There was no point in trying to hide it any longer; he had been found out.

'I'm sorry,' he said. 'I was out of order. I was concerned about you but I can understand why you might be angry with me.'

'I'm not angry, Matty lad. Disappointed that you did not trust me, maybe.' Harris gave the sergeant a reassuring look. 'Let's draw a line under it, shall we? We have more important things to worry about.'

‘Fair enough.’ Gallagher tried not to let his relief show but was aware that the pounding of his heart had eased. ‘So, had you got anywhere with Geoff?’

‘I was getting closer. We had more whisky than was healthy at his place in Tenter Street one night last week and he said a few things that suggested he was worried about being into something heavy. He’d have slipped up sometime, I think.’

‘But then someone shot him.’

‘But then someone shot him.’

* * *

Bernard Joffey watched in silence from his office window as the car approached along the drive that led up to the country house hotel a few miles outside Levton Bridge. The vehicle pulled up outside The Hillview Hotel and two young people got out, a slim, dark-haired man and a short-haired blonde woman in a dark suit. The general manager did not recognise the man but he knew that the woman was Detective Constable Alison Butterfield. He headed out of his office and down the corridor to the front lobby where the new arrivals were talking to the receptionist.

‘I’ll deal with this, Melanie,’ said Joffey. He extended a hand in welcome to Butterfield.

‘Good to see you again, Alison,’ he said. ‘How’s your dad? We haven’t seen him and your mum for a while.’

‘His arthritis is getting worse, I am afraid, Bernard. He doesn’t get out much. He gave the farm up at the right time.’

‘Well, send him my regards, will you?’ Joffey turned to the young man and offered him his hand. ‘I don’t think we’ve met. Bernard Joffey, General Manager.’

‘DC Alistair Marshall,’ said the man as they shook hands. The constable glanced at the receptionist, who was listening to the conversation. ‘Can we go somewhere private to talk, do you think, Mr Joffey?’

'Sure.' Joffey led the detectives into his office and gestured for them to sit on the sofa in the window. He sat down in an armchair. 'Is this about what happened last night?'

'Sort of,' said Butterfield. 'We want to find out more about the incident a few days ago involving Bill Harding from the Hewby Moor Estate and a bird club member called Pete Guthrie.'

'Unpleasant business,' said Joffey. He shook his head. 'Bill was having dinner with his wife and children and Guthrie came storming over and started shouting about the hen harriers. You know what he's like. A real hothead. Said there'd be hell to pay if anyone harmed the chicks. The language was appalling. The kids looked really frightened.'

'And what did Bill Harding do?' asked Marshall.

'You know Bill. He stayed calm like he always does.'

'And you did not report the incident to us?' asked Butterfield.

'That's for Bill to do. There was no way I was going to do it. The last thing I wanted was for it to go to court and get reported in the paper.' Joffey gave a slight smile. 'I've just paid through the nose for a new marketing strategy and, oddly enough, the people who wrote it did not mention having customers being harangued as a good subject for an advert.'

The detectives smiled at the joke. Joffey's next comment wiped the smile from their faces.

'Actually, I'm rather surprised that you didn't come here last night,' said Joffey. 'Given that the chap who was killed was with Pete Guthrie the night the incident with the Hardings happened.'

The detectives stared at him in astonishment.

'Geoff Morden was here?' said Marshall.

'Yes. I thought that was why you were here. Him and Pete had been having a drink in the lounge before the trouble began.'

'And did Geoff take part in the altercation?' asked Butterfield.

'No, he stayed in the lounge but he left with Pete after it happened.' The general manager smiled at them. 'But I'm forgetting my manners. I should have offered you a cup of tea.'

* * *

'So, tell me about Ged Rutherford,' said Gallagher as the car passed a sign indicating that the southbound M6 was just three miles away. 'Is he easy to work with?'

'He won't be when he finds out about MI5,' said Harris. 'He'll be furious that he's been kept in the dark. It was always his big criticism of me.'

'You didn't get on with him then?'

'It's complicated.'

'It usually is with you,' said Gallagher.

Harris did not reply. Not a man given to talking about himself, he took the view that he had already offered enough information for one day. However, he knew Gallagher well enough to know that he would not stop badgering his boss until he had an answer. In Harris's experience of car journeys with Matty Gallagher, the sergeant had an intense dislike of silence.

'It was more than ten years ago,' said Harris. 'I'd not been with Greater Manchester that long but I'd already made DS and the top brass thought it would be a good idea to pair me and Ged up in a new team to tackle organised crime in the city. They said they'd make me up to Acting Detective Inspector, if I agreed to head it up.'

'Sounds like a big ask for someone who had not long been a DS.'

'It was but none of the more experienced officers fancied it. The job was seen as a career-breaker, if it went wrong. Ged fancied it, though, and he refused to serve under me. Said he couldn't work under an officer with less years on the force than him. He seemed to forget that I'd also done ten years in the Army. Anyway, in the end, the brass had to order him. He's never forgiven me.'

'I assume it worked, though?'

'Too right it did,' said Harris. 'Ged knew about as much about the gangs as I did and, to be fair to him, he never let me down. Eventually, they offered me DCI, still in charge of the team, but that was the last straw and Ged demanded a transfer. He was delighted when I turned the promotion down to come up here instead.'

'And he took over from you, did he?'

'Not immediately, no. He went off and did the promotion thing then they brought him back to lead the unit as part of a reorganisation. He's doing a good job, from what I hear from Leckie.'

'And Lynton Jago, who's he?' asked Gallagher.

'He's bad news, that's what he is,' said Harris with a scowl. 'Drugs. Protection. Extortion. The lot. The man's a psychopath and he's perfectly capable of organising a hit if Geoff did fall foul of him – and he won't like the idea of me being back in Manchester either. Here's the junction.'

Gallagher slowed down for a small roundabout then guided his car down onto the motorway slip road.

'So, just to make sure that I have got this right,' he said when they had joined the southbound carriageway. 'We're going to meet a DCI who detests you to discuss a psychopath who loathes you and an MI5 officer whom you may or may not have slept with?'

'When you say it like that, it's not complicated at all, is it?' Harris gave a slight smile. 'Put your foot down, Lewis. We don't want to be late.'

Chapter sixteen

Gillian Roberts looked across her desk at the dark-haired woman in her thirties who had just sat down. Linda Morden's eyes were dark and hooded and the smudged make-up and the traces of tears on her cheeks were testament to the strong emotions she was experiencing following the death of her father. Her hands constantly twisted and untwisted a damp handkerchief. It was all very convincing, thought Roberts, she was doing everything right, and yet… and yet… something nagged away at the back of the detective inspector's mind. She had seen more victims than enough down the years and they all had an unmistakable raw quality, a sense of emotion stripped bare, an authenticity that could not be faked, and none of that was present, in Roberts' view. She could not resist the thought that she was witnessing a carefully constructed façade.

Roberts resolved to keep her suspicions to herself in view of Harris's final words before he left for his meeting. *Just act as you would normally.* Maybe, thought the detective inspector, as she watched Linda dab her eyes with the handkerchief again, she was allowing her view to be twisted by the allegations against her father. Maybe Linda knew nothing about firearms being transported halfway across Europe in one of the company's trucks. And, Roberts reminded herself, Linda's father *had* been murdered, after all. Like it or not, she was a victim. With that thought, the mother in Roberts forced its way to the surface, as it always did.

'Can I get you a cup of coffee, lovey?' she asked. 'It might make you feel better.'

'No, thanks,' said Linda. 'The radio said that you think my father was killed by accident? Something to do with protecting the birds. Is that true?'

'It's one of the theories we're working on, yes.' *Just act as you would normally*. 'However, we can't rule out the possibility that it was deliberate.'

'Deliberate?' Tears threatened to bubble up again. 'Why would anyone want to kill Dad?'

Roberts watched as Linda dabbed her eyes with her soggy handkerchief. If it's an act, it's a damned good one, she thought. Her attitude towards Linda continued to soften.

'That's what we need to find out,' she said. 'Had your father mentioned any reservations about guarding the birds?'

'No, he was really keen to do it. He'd talked about little else since he heard that the female was sitting on eggs.' Linda smiled. 'He was crazy about birds, was Dad. He spent his childhood in the hills around here, did you know that? Collecting eggs with Jack Harris. Dad said that they were among the happiest days of his life. I thought that Jack might have been here to see me.'

'Sorry, but he's been called away.'

'The radio said that he is leading the investigation into my father's death.'

'He is, yes,' said Roberts. 'Tell me, did you father ever say that he was–'

'No offence, but I would rather talk to Jack. He was one of my father's oldest friends and I think that I would feel more comfortable with him.'

'I am afraid that won't be possible, lovey. You'll have to make do with me.'

'Of course. I'm sorry. I didn't mean to offend.'

They were the right words, thought Roberts, but she could not help thinking that they were delivered in the wrong way. Again, she found herself entertaining suspicions about Linda Morden. Again, she did not show her concerns.

'That's alright,' said the inspector instead. 'You're under a lot of strain. So, just to be clear, your father was not worried about guarding the nest?'

'If he was, he never mentioned it and we talked on the phone most days after he came to live up here.'

'Yes, tell me about the move up here,' said Roberts. 'He was building a house, wasn't he?'

'It had been his dream for years,' said Linda. Again, she smiled. It seemed genuine. 'He got the idea from that *Grand Designs* programme. He'd seen a house with turrets and said that he'd always fancied something like that. He said that he would love Kevin McCloud to come and make a programme about it.'

'Why make the move now?' asked Roberts.

'He'd worked hard for thirty years and said it was about time that he spent some of his money. He'd made a lot of money from Speedwagonz, had Dad.'

'Do you think it is possible that he could have also made enemies?'

Linda looked surprised.

'Why should he?' she asked.

'Well, it's a competitive business and Speedwagonz does have a bit of a reputation, does it not?' Roberts glanced at the notepad on the table. 'Several of your drivers have ended up in court.'

'Only on minor traffic offences.' Linda Morden stiffened. 'And I don't see what that has got to do with what happened to Dad.'

'Might any of the other company owners have wanted to see your father harmed?'

'I wouldn't have thought so.'

'So, what about–'

'I'm sorry, Detective Inspector, but I am finding these questions very upsetting.'

'I appreciate that,' said Roberts. 'But they have to be asked.'

'Look, I'm not pretending that there have not been moments of tension with other company owners from time to time,' said Linda. 'It's the nature of the business but none of them would have hurt my father. I'm sure of that.'

'Who inherits Speedwagonz now that your father is dead?'

The question seemed to startle Linda.

'Why does that matter?' she asked. 'What are you suggesting?'

'I'm not suggesting anything. Just answer the question, please.'

'If you must know, Speedwagonz has three shareholders.' Linda seemed wary. 'Dad had 51 per cent of the shares and I have 29 per cent.'

'Siblings?'

'I'm an only child.'

'Husband?' asked Roberts.

'I'm not married.'

'Boyfriend?'

'I'm single,' said Linda.

'So, who owns the other 20 per cent of the company?'

'The finance director. Gary Nesbitt. He's been with Dad pretty much from the start.'

'And would I be right in assuming that ownership of Speedwagonz passes to the two of you now that your father is dead, with you as the major shareholder?' asked Roberts.

'If you are trying to suggest that we had something to do with the death of my…' Linda Morden did not complete the sentence and sat back and crossed her arms. 'Sorry, but I'll only talk to Jack.'

'As you wish,' said Roberts. 'Let's end it there then, shall we?'

* * *

A couple of minutes later, Linda was taken to a washroom by a female constable so that she could freshen up before the journey down the valley to Roxham where she would identify her father's body at the general hospital's mortuary. When she had gone, Roberts closed her office door, picked up her mobile phone from the desk and prepared to call Harris. Thought of the DCI brought forth a frown. Roberts knew that she had done the right thing in bringing Gallagher's concerns to the attention of the divisional commander but was also acutely aware that she should have had more faith in Harris. The realisation troubled her. She made the call.

'Gillian,' said the inspector's voice. She could hear the sound of the car's engine in the background. 'How'd it go with Linda?'

'Not good. She got really uptight when I asked her who inherited the company. Call me suspicious but we can't escape the fact that whoever killed her father made her a very wealthy woman. And now she says she'll only talk to you. Says she'll be at the house in Tenter Street later.'

'I'll pop round,' said Harris. 'Do you think she knows anything about the firearms?'

'Difficult to say and obviously I did not mention it.'

'Fair enough,' said Harris. 'Anything else happening?'

'An interesting snippet. Alison has been on from The Hillview. According to the general manager, Geoff

Morden was there the night that Guthrie had his bust-up with Bill Harding.'

'He would seem to have had a knack for being in the wrong place at the wrong time, would our Geoff,' said Harris.

* * *

After a morning of intense questioning, a stressed George Matthews was returned to the dimly lit room at the Organised Crime Unit's headquarters.

'Can I get you anything?' asked Gerry Bayliss as he gestured for Matthews to take a seat. He glanced at the wall clock, which read eleven forty-five. 'Lunch, maybe? There's a chuck wagon comes round about twelve. It does excellent sandwiches.'

'No, thanks.'

'You really should eat something, George. Like I said earlier, you're going to need all your strength.'

'I'm alright,' said Matthews. 'What happens to me now?'

'It's yet to be decided. The governor has had to go to another meeting and has ordered that you be kept here until he gets back. He'll make up his mind then.'

'And Esther. When can I see her?'

'Maybe tonight.'

'How is she?' asked Matthews.

'Upset.'

There was a knock on the door and the burly, unsmiling officer walked in and glanced at Bayliss.

'Can I have a word?' he asked.

The two men walked out into the corridor. Several minutes later Bayliss was back, this time with a grave expression on his face.

'What's wrong?' asked Matthews anxiously.

'It's nothing to worry about.'

'Why don't I believe you?'

Bayliss sighed.

'Look, I didn't want to mention this before,' he said. 'But a couple of Jago's men tried to follow us when we left the safe house this morning. We headed them off but their car has just pulled up at the end of the road. We'll get it moved on but, clearly, they know where you are.'

'But how could that have happened?' asked Matthews anxiously.

'It's a good question.' Bayliss glanced up at the wall clock again. 'You should definitely eat something. I can recommend the ham.'

Chapter seventeen

Having left the M6, Matty Gallagher drove a short distance along the side road that ran behind the motorway services, then turned his vehicle into the car park next to the small hotel. After getting out and glancing round to make sure that they were not being watched – both he and Harris were on high alert now that the stakes seemed so much higher – the two detectives walked over to the building.

'Not looking forward to this,' said Gallagher.

'Why not?'

Gallagher hesitated, wondering whether he should have spoken given their recent disagreement. Harris stopped walking and looked at him.

'Well?' said the inspector. 'Why not?'

'Because it smacks of politics,' said Gallagher. 'And you've never been good at politics.'

'What is this?' said the inspector. 'Open season on Jack Harris?'

'I'm sorry, I didn't mean to…'

'But you're right.' Harris started walking again. 'And I'm sure you'll keep me correct. That big city experience you keep telling me about.'

The quip brought forth a small sigh of relief from Gallagher and he followed his boss out of the bright summer sunshine into the shade of the building. They headed through the reception area, casting a glance at the bored-looking receptionist reading a magazine behind the desk, and walked along one of the ground floor corridors towards room eleven, as instructed by Rutherford. Harris knocked on the door, which was opened by Jenny Armannsson.

'Hello, love,' she said.

She gave Harris a peck on the cheek as he entered the room. The inspector did not reciprocate, embarrassed at the gesture and determined to keep things professional. Gallagher noticed his discomfort and he and Armannsson exchanged amused glances.

'No kiss for me then?' said Gallagher.

'Behave yourself,' said Armannsson.

Gallagher chuckled, walked over to the man sitting at the low table in the window and extended a hand in welcome. 'Detective Sergeant Gallagher, sir, good to meet you.'

'Sergeant.' Rutherford stood up and shook the hand then awkwardly extended a hand of welcome to Harris as well. 'Long time no see, Jack. Never thought it would take Lynton Jago to bring us back together.'

'Indeed. How did you explain our presence to the receptionist?'

'She thinks we're a double-glazing sales team.' There was a knock on the door. Rutherford tensed and gave the Levton Bridge detectives a sharp look. 'Were you followed? Because if you were…'

'Relax, we weren't followed,' said Harris calmly.

He opened the door and a slim, smartly dressed, dark-haired woman in her mid-thirties walked into the room.

'Hello, Susan,' said Harris.

'Hello, Jack.'

Rutherford glowered at Harris.

'What the hell is she doing here?' he asked suspiciously.

'And hello to you, Ged,' said Peters.

'You never change, do you, Jack?' said Rutherford. He gave an angry shake of the head. 'Always playing by your own rules. You should have told me that MI5 were involved.'

'And me,' said Armannsson. She gave Harris a reproachful look. 'You should have told me.'

'It was on a need-to-know basis,' said Harris.

'Well, if that's the way you want to play it,' said Rutherford. He picked his file up off the table and stood up to leave.

'Sit down, Ged,' said Peters. Her voice had an air of authority about it. 'It was me who told Jack not to say anything so, if you want to blame anyone, you can blame me.'

She gestured to the teapot on the table.

'Anything left in that?' she asked. 'I'm parched.'

Rutherford stood for a few moments, deciding whether or not he should follow through with his threat to leave the room, then sighed, placed the file back on the table and walked over to the phone on the bedside table. Having grudgingly rung room service, he returned to his seat. Everyone else sat down as well – Harris and Peters on the other chairs clustered round the table, Gallagher and Armannsson perched on the edge of the bed. The atmosphere crackled with tension.

'This is nice,' said Peters brightly.

'You've got ten minutes,' said Rutherford. 'I don't like being played for a fool.'

'Which is exactly what Jack said,' replied Peters.

Rutherford seemed mollified by the comment and glanced at Harris, recognising that they had something in common. He knew only too well from bitter experience how it felt to deal with the security services and it was not the first time that he had found his inquiries into organised crime in the Manchester area complicated by their involvement. Harris sensed what he was thinking and shrugged. Despite his irritation, Rutherford gave a slight smile. A fleeting moment of connection between two former colleagues.

'So, what's this about?' asked Rutherford.

'Four months ago,' said Peters, 'one of our people picked up some information of interest about Kosovo. Do you know much about Kosovo, Ged?'

'Not really.' Rutherford knew that it was a rhetorical question and knew why it had been asked. He detested the way that it put him at a disadvantage. 'But then I suspect you know that.'

'Well, suffice to say that it has been a delicate political situation there for a long time. Our informant heard that a splinter group is seeking to seize power and plans to raise the cash to do it by selling stolen army issue firearms abroad, namely here in the UK.'

'Selling to whom?' asked Rutherford. His irritation was receding rapidly as the ramifications played out in his mind. The machinations of MI5 he did not always understand, illegally trafficked firearms he did.

'It would seem that they have found a buyer in the far-right movement over here,' said Peters. 'Ourselves and Counter Terrorism have been tracking several groups for a while and there's a link with one, in particular. We don't know an awful lot about them, to be honest, but they appear to be small, hard-line and extremely well organised – and they're talking on a regular basis to similar groups in America.'

'Where are they based?' asked Rutherford.

'From what we can gather, they are run by a couple of guys in Hertfordshire, an IT specialist who has his own small business and a council clerk. They've also got members in the North. Sheffield, Leeds, Bradford.'

'Do we know why they need the weapons?' asked Armannsson.

'We understand that they are planning a series of attacks on high-profile targets to draw attention to their cause,' said Peters. 'Rather like what happened at Westminster Bridge.'

'And they can pull off something like that, can they?' said Rutherford.

'They can with a load of ex-army weapons, Ged. Previously, these types of groups have tended to be all talk and no action beyond a few demos but this lot are different. They believe in race war and we're pretty sure that they are prepared to follow through on their plans. I don't need to tell you that poses a serious terrorist threat.'

'And we are involved how?' asked Rutherford. His grudging tone had been replaced by something more professional. Urgent.

'According to our informant, the Kosovans plan to bring the arms into the UK on a Speedwagonz truck. A number of their lorries do regular runs to and from Kosovo but our informant does not know which driver is involved. That is why we were so interested in Geoff Morden. Jack had been asked to find out more if he could.'

'Why him?' asked Rutherford. He glanced suspiciously at Harris, old rivalries resurfacing. 'Speedwagonz are a Manchester company. We could have sorted out a covert op.'

'I am sure you could but Geoff had moved to Jack's area. Besides, they had known each other for many years. It was too good an opportunity to turn down. In addition, Jack has some knowledge of Kosovo.' Peters gave Rutherford a sly look. 'He wouldn't need to look on a map to find out where it is. And he already had a particular reason for being involved. Do you want to tell him, Jack?'

Harris hesitated.

'It's personal,' he said

'I think it might help Ged understand a little better,' said Peters. 'Give him an idea why you were so keen to help.'

Harris sighed.

'If you insist,' he said. 'My involvement dates back to 1998, Ged. From when I was in the Army and serving with the United Nations peacekeeping force at the time of the civil war in Kosovo. It was a brutal conflict and some terrible things were done.'

The inspector was silent for a few moments as his mind went back to a clearing in a dank forest in the Drenica region. He recalled again the chill as dusk brought with it a heavy silence; there were no birds singing that evening as he and his comrades stood and stared at the bodies strewn in front of houses that had been set alight as the village was destroyed.

'I was part of a team that had been sent to investigate reports of a massacre,' he said. 'There were fifteen bodies when we arrived. Most of them were adults but there were four children. They had been stabbed multiple times.'

The room was silent as the others gave him time to gather his thoughts. Even though they had seen numerous bodies in their careers, the thought of children always took things up another level. Rutherford thought of his two boys and Susan Peters of her daughter.

'There were three girls and one boy,' said Harris quietly. 'None of them was aged more than fourteen. I heard later that one of them was only ten. The pathologist reckoned that some of them would have taken several hours to bleed to death. He reckoned that was the idea. None of the wounds would have been fatal in themselves.'

'Jesus,' said Rutherford.

Although Jenny Armannsson had heard the story before, she reached into her handbag and produced a handkerchief with which she dabbed her eyes.

'I'd tried to put it to the back of mind for years,' continued Harris. He seemed almost unaware that they were there, and his eyes appeared to focus on the middle distance out of the window. 'Then a few months ago, I was approached to give a statement for use in a prosecution being brought by the International Criminal Court.'

Gallagher looked at his boss with concern; he knew that Harris had been struggling with the memories since the request had been made and had undergone several sessions with a counsellor. The revelation that his boss had sought help had surprised the sergeant, given Harris's bullish approach to personal matters.

'The prosecutors have identified the man who ordered the killings,' said Harris. 'It's the same man that Susan's informant says is leading the coup.'

'He's been under surveillance for some time,' said Peters. 'Once we have seized the firearms, the Kosovan police will arrest him.'

Rutherford was silent for a few moments.

'I can't compete with that,' he said eventually. 'But it would still have helped if we'd known about it.'

'I couldn't risk it,' said Peters.

'Why not?' Rutherford fixed her with a hard stare. 'Don't you trust us?'

'The fewer people know about this the better, Ged, but I have to admit to being intrigued by a possible link with Lynton Jago. We suspected that someone had put together the deal and there's not much to connect Speedwagonz directly with the far-right group. How come you think there's a connection with the death of Geoff Morden?'

Rutherford told them about George Matthews.

'Whichever way you look at it,' he said in conclusion, 'this is one for Organised Crime. Jack, I am sure that you and your team can be useful in assisting our inquiries but–'

'*Your* inquiries?' said Harris. 'What about *our* inquiries?'

'With all due respect, this is too big for you. You can feed whatever you find into our investigation.'

'No way,' said Harris.

'Come on, Jack,' protested Rutherford, 'Organised Crime in a big city force against CID in a small rural division with more sheep than people? There's no competition, surely?'

Gallagher held his breath and waited for the explosion. He knew how Harris detested anyone who tried to unfavourably compare officers in Levton Bridge with their urban counterparts. When the riposte came from Harris, though, it was delivered in a quiet, controlled voice.

'There is no way I am working for you,' he said. Harris stood up and prepared to leave the room. 'And that's final.'

'You never did have much of a sense of irony, did you?' said Rutherford. He gave the inspector a sly look. 'I seem to recall you objecting when I used the same words all those years ago. You spouted some management guff about us all working as a team, I seem to remember.'

Susan Peters had listened to the exchange with a faint air of amusement but noting the rise in tension again, she sighed and held up a hand.

'Children, children,' she said. 'If I may resolve this dispute. You'll both be working for me. National Security trumps Plod.'

Both Rutherford and Harris opened their mouths to reply but there was a knock on the door before either of them could speak. Peters smiled brightly.

'That'll be the tea,' she said. 'Excellent.'

* * *

Thirty minutes later, Harris and Gallagher were in the sergeant's car as it headed back towards the M6.

'Politics,' said Gallagher. He glanced across at his boss. 'Who needs it, eh?'

Harris did not reply; he was still fuming at Rutherford's attempt to hijack the investigation.

'Mind, she's a tough cookie that Susan Peters,' said the sergeant.

Realising, as ever, that the sergeant would not let the subject drop, Harris nodded.

'She's always known what she wants,' Harris said. 'And she usually gets it.'

'Oh, aye?' grinned Gallagher.

'I told you–' said Harris but before he could say anything else his mobile phone rang. He put it on speaker so that Gallagher could hear.

'You OK to talk?' said Roberts' voice.

'Yeah, just finished.'

'How did it go with the spooks?'

'Tetchy.'

'And Ged Rutherford?'

'Tried to sideline us,' said Harris. 'He thinks it's one for Organised Crime.'

'In which case, he may wish to reconsider the old truth that, more often than not, murder is closer to home than you might think.'

'Why, what you got?'

'Your pal Pete Guthrie has just turned up at the Hewby Moor Estate, shouting off his mouth and telling anyone who will listen that Bill Harding killed Geoff. And it would seem that he ignored your advice about not taking the law into his own hands. According to the estate office, he's got a baseball bat.'

'We got folks on the way?'

'Uniform have sent a car and Alison and Alistair were heading there anyway to interview Bill Harding about what happened at The Hillview. When will you be back?'

'An hour, maybe.' Harris glanced at Gallagher. 'If Lewis Hamilton puts his foot down.'

Gallagher grinned and did as he was told. As the car jumped forward, Harris replaced the phone in the glove compartment. It rang again.

'Bloody hell,' exclaimed the inspector. He took it back out of the compartment. 'No peace for the wicked.'

'Who is it?' asked Gallagher as he eased the car onto the northbound carriageway of the motorway

'Number withheld.'

‘Perhaps they’re trying to sell you some double glazing.’

‘Perhaps they are.’ The inspector smiled at the joke and put the call on speaker. ‘Hello, DCI Jack Harris.’

‘Jack, it’s Ged.’ The DCI sounded uneasy. Embarrassed even. ‘Look, I need a favour.’

‘What, from little old us?’

‘Don’t make this more difficult than it already is. It would seem that our security has been compromised. It looks like Jago’s people know where we’ve been keeping George Matthews.’

‘How did that happen?’ asked Harris.

‘I wish I knew but our Witness Protection people are running round like headless chickens and say that they can’t take Matthews on until they’re satisfied that we haven’t had a breach. I have to get him away from Manchester pretty damn quick. I don’t suppose you have a remote farmhouse lying empty, do you? Somewhere he can hide out for a couple of days until I get something sorted?’

‘With plenty of sheep?’ said Harris.

He winked at Gallagher, who gave a low laugh.

‘You do know that I hate you, don’t you?’ said Rutherford.

‘I’ll get back to you,’ said Harris. He ended the call and looked across at Gallagher. ‘And that, is why Susan Peters did not want to involve Organised Crime.’

Chapter eighteen

Alison Butterfield and Alistair Marshall were the first to arrive at the Hewby Moor Estate following the 999 call, the detectives' car speeding into the yard in a shower of gravel, followed by a fast-moving patrol vehicle, driven by PC Leslie Jardine, with its blue light flashing. The officers got out of their vehicles to be confronted by the sight of a wide-eyed Pete Guthrie prowling round the yard and wielding his baseball bat while terrified staff cowered in the nearby stables. One of the young female stable hands was in tears and being comforted by an older colleague.

Guthrie whirled round to face the new threat and the officers could see that the veins on his neck were bulging and that his grip on the bat had tightened. Guthrie jabbed the weapon in their direction.

'You stay out of this!' he snarled.

'I am afraid we can't do that,' said Butterfield. 'Drop the bat.'

'Stay back!' yelled Guthrie as the officers started to approach him. 'Or so help me, I'll hurt someone!'

Marshall and Jardine stopped walking and Butterfield noticed that Henry Masterson was standing at the door to one of the stables in urgent conversation with a man wearing a green tweed suit and with grey hair poking out from beneath his flat cap. She recognised him as the estate manager Bill Harding. Leaving Marshall and Jardine to keep an eye on Guthrie, the young constable walked over to the two men.

'This is your doing,' said Masterson before she could speak. He gave her an accusing look. 'He's crazy enough without you spreading all those half-truths about us.'

'Only half?' said Butterfield and instantly regretted the words.

Masterson glared at her furiously.

'That's just the kind of comment we can do without,' he said. 'This has been handled appallingly.'

'I was just doing my job,' said Butterfield.

'Your job is not to put ideas into the head of crackerjacks like Pete Guthrie! I mean, look at the man – he's bloody deranged.'

As Guthrie continued to brandish the bat, Marshall and Jardine exchanged nods and started approaching him again, moving slowly and carefully. When they were a few metres away, they stopped walking and Marshall held out his hand.

'Give me the bat, Pete,' he said. 'This is only making things worse.'

Guthrie glanced at Masterson and Harding.

'I'm doing nothing until you arrest them,' he said.

'For what?' asked Marshall.

'You know damned well what for!' exclaimed Guthrie. 'For killing Geoff.'

'On what evidence?' asked Marshall.

'You know they did it.'

'Even if I believed that, I'd need evidence,' said Marshall. He took another couple of steps forward. 'I believe that DCI Harris keeps telling you that.'

'Harris doesn't care,' said Guthrie with a derisory snort. He held up the bat. 'Stay back!'

Marshall stopped walking again. The detective constable was acutely conscious that, young as he was, he was still the senior officer on the scene and that he needed to take the lead. Masterson noticed Marshall's hesitation.

'I've had enough of this rubbish,' he said in a voice that was loud enough for Guthrie to hear. 'The man's a fucking lunatic. Are you going to arrest him or not?'

Guthrie roared with anger and started to run towards the estate owner, brandishing the bat. The movement was all that Alistair Marshall required. With his hesitation banished and Guthrie distracted, the detective darted forwards and rugby-tackled him, bringing him crashing to the ground. Guthrie gave a loud grunt of pain and lost hold of the bat. The two men struggled on the ground for a few moments until Guthrie squealed as Marshall twisted his arms behind his back and applied the handcuffs. Within moments, Jardine was by their side and Guthrie had been hauled roughly to his feet and was struggling to free himself.

'Calm down!' said Marshall.

Guthrie struggled for a few more seconds but, as Marshall twisted his arms again, sending daggers of pain shooting up to his shoulder, he realised the hopelessness of his position and stood still.

'That's better,' said Marshall.

Masterson strode over and jabbed a finger at Guthrie.

'I want him charged,' he said. 'He can't go around terrifying my staff like that. What happened at The Hillview was bad enough.'

Butterfield walked up to them.

'What's this about, Pete?' she asked.

'The birds have gone,' said Guthrie. The fight had left him and he appeared to be close to tears. 'All the disturbance has driven them from the nest.'

'You and those bloody birds,' said Masterson dismissively.

'Yes, well, you've got what you wanted now, haven't you?' said Guthrie. The fire was back in his eyes and he turned to face the approaching Bill Harding. 'Both of you have. Everyone knows that you never wanted the harriers here. All you care about is your precious grouse. Blood money, that's what it is.'

'Whether I wanted them here or not is irrelevant,' said Masterson. 'You have come here making wild accusations about me and Bill, and you'll pay for it.'

He looked expectantly at the detectives.

'Won't he?' he added.

'He'll be interviewed, yes,' said Butterfield.

'Well, he'll better be charged as well!'

'I can assure you that things will be done properly,' said Butterfield as Marshall led Pete Guthrie to the patrol car. 'Is this true about the birds, Henry?'

'It is, yes, but you needn't go thinking it's anything to do with us. No, it's your people tramping around up there that drove them away. See what Jack Harris makes of that, why don't you?' Masterson looked at her suspiciously. 'And how come you got here so quickly, anyway? Is the estate under surveillance, because if it is…'

'It isn't. We've just come from The Hillview Hotel. The general manager told us that Geoff Morden was with Pete Guthrie the night Bill and his family were threatened.' She turned to Harding. 'Is that true, Bill?'

'What if it is?'

'Just answer the question. Was Geoff Morden there?'

'He was, yes,' said Harding.

'Any idea what sparked the trouble?' asked Butterfield.

'The man's a crackerjack,' said Masterson. 'That's what sparked the trouble.'

'You weren't there, Henry. I'm asking Bill.'

Harding hesitated.

'Guthrie might have thought that I was laughing at him,' he said eventually.

'And were you?'

'Who cares if he was?' exclaimed Masterton, who could not contain his fury. He gestured to Marshall and Jardine as they put Guthrie into the back of the patrol vehicle. 'Why are you giving Bill a hard time? Guthrie's the one you should be hassling.'

'Yes, but we have to understand why he is saying that someone from the estate shot Geoff Morden,' said Butterfield.

'I have already warned you, young lady. All these insinuations are out of order. After this, I will be straight onto your chief constable. I take it you know that he sometimes comes shooting up here?'

'Do what you want,' said Butterfield.

'Oh, I will. And I don't need your permission to do it either.'

Butterfield watched Masterson walk into the stables with a look of resignation on her face. It wouldn't be the first formal complaint that she had received in her fledgling CID career. Far from it. Normally, they happened when she allowed her desire to impress senior officers to get the better of her. Gallagher was constantly warning her to think before she spoke. However, this time, she knew that she had done the right thing. Harris had always told her that it was important to do the job without fear or favour, particularly in a valley where everyone knew everyone else's business. And something about Henry Masterson's belligerence was troubling the young constable.

'I wouldn't worry,' said Harding, breaking into her thoughts. 'Henry's just upset.'

'I appreciate that, Bill. However–'

'But he's right. If you keep suggesting that we are somehow involved in the death of Geoff Morden, you're asking for a load of trouble.' There was an edge to Harding's voice now. 'He's got a lot of influential friends, has Henry Masterson. And not just your chief constable.'

'What does that mean?'

'Just that it's worth remembering before you let your mouth run away with you.'

Harding walked over to join Masterson at the stables. Butterfield watched him go with an uneasy expression on her face. Courteous as Bill Harding usually was, the meaning behind the comment had been clear. Deep in thought, the constable walked over to the patrol car, where Marshall was leaning on the bonnet. He noted her troubled expression.

'You OK?' he asked.

'I've just been threatened,' she said in a low voice.

'That's just Henry Masterson shooting his mouth off like he usually does,' said Marshall. 'I wouldn't worry about it.'

'By Bill Harding.'

'Really?' Marshall looked surprised. 'That's not his style.'

'There's something not right here, Alistair.' Butterfield walked up to the rear passenger door and leaned into the car. 'What makes you say that they killed Geoff, Pete?'

'Like you care.'

'Humour me,' said Butterfield.

'Why should I? None of you want to know. Jack Harris certainly doesn't.'

'What if I said that I was prepared to believe you?' asked Butterfield. 'Have you got more than just wild accusations? Do you have anything to prove them?'

'I just know it.'

'Evidence, Pete,' said Butterfield. 'Where's the evidence?'

Guthrie did not reply.

'No, I thought not,' said Butterfield. She looked at Jardine, who was in the driver's seat. 'You OK to take him down to the station, Leslie?'

'Sure,' said Jardine.

* * *

Back at Levton Bridge Police Station, it was mid-afternoon and Gillian Roberts was in her office, trying not to feel old as she looked at the young woman with the fresh complexion and close-cropped dark hair who was sitting on the other side of the desk. Sally Orr returned the gaze uneasily; it was the young detective constable's first murder inquiry and she was terrified that she would make a mistake. Everyone knew that Jack Harris and the other senior officers expected the very highest standards from their detectives and that the DCI took a dim view of those who failed to live up to them.

Orr was twenty-four and had been a detective for just three weeks, one of a number of young officers to join CID at Levton Bridge over the previous eight months. Harris had asked headquarters for someone more experienced to fill the latest vacancy in order to restore the balance of the team but had, to his disgust, been told that there was a shortage of available senior officers and that he was being offered Sally Orr instead. Headquarters' insistence that she had potential had done little to improve to improve Harris's mood and he had put the phone down, looked across his desk at Roberts and muttered something about 'bleeding nursemaids'. Roberts was keeping a close eye on Orr to ensure that she did not do anything to attract the DCI's disapproval. The role had brought out her motherly instincts, as it always did when she dealt with young officers.

'So, lovey,' said the detective inspector. She gestured to the piece of paper in the constable's hand. 'You got the statement from Harry Groves OK then?'

'I did, yes, ma'am.'

'Any problems?'

'No, it was all straightforward, like you said it would be. Took a bit longer than I thought it would because he took several calls on his mobile. To do with his work.'

'He's a busy man is Harry Groves, particularly in the summer,' said Roberts. 'He's a handyman, works for local property owners, holiday lets, that sort of thing. So, what did he say?'

'Just repeated the story he has already told us.'

'And he remains convinced that it was an attack on the nest, does he?'

'He does, yes, ma'am,' said Orr. 'He doesn't believe that anyone would set out to kill Geoff Morden deliberately.'

'They know each other of old, I think?'

'They went to the same schools, yes, but they hadn't seen each other for the best part of three decades. They only met up again when Geoff returned to Levton Bridge. Harry did say that Geoff had been a bit distracted in recent days.'

'Did he say why?'

'Harry thought it was the idea of guarding the nest. He said that all the bird club people felt the same. That someone might try something.'

'That all he was worried about?' asked Roberts.

'It's all Harry could think of.' Orr looked worried. 'Have I missed something, ma'am? I got him to mention it in his statement.'

Roberts gestured for her to hand over the document and Orr slid it across the desk. The constable watched anxiously as Roberts read it through then gave a slight sigh of relief as the detective inspector nodded and placed the document back on the desk.

'It seems pretty straightforward to me,' she said. 'OK, go and get a cuppa and something to eat. You can leave the statement. I'll sort it. I'll catch up with you later.'

After Orr had left the room, Roberts picked up the document and thoughtfully scanned it again.

'Perhaps it is to do with the birds, after all,' she murmured.

She remembered that Alison Butterfield had asked to see her when she had a free moment, so she stood up and walked along the corridor to the CID room where

Butterfield and Marshall were sitting at their desks, writing up their notes.

'You interviewed Guthrie yet?' asked Roberts.

She took a seat and felt suddenly weary as her lack of sleep caught up with her. The detective inspector glanced up at the wall clock and wondered when she'd be able to leave for home.

'We've just finished,' said Marshall.

'And?'

'He's sticking to his story that someone from the estate shot Geoff Morden. Trouble is, he's got nothing to back it up. It's all talk.'

'And what do you think?' asked Roberts.

'I think he's upset,' said Marshall. 'He was good friends with Geoff Morden and I think that he's lashing out – he's after someone to blame. Henry Masterson is the obvious one on whom to take his anger out.'

'You could be right,' said Roberts.

'What do you want us to do with him?' asked Marshall.

'Keep him in overnight. Give him time to cool off. The last thing we want is Pete Guthrie going back to Hewby Moor, the mood he's in. What did you want to see me about, Alison?'

Butterfield hesitated and glanced at Marshall.

'Well?' said Roberts.

'Is there something that we are not being told?' said the constable eventually.

'What makes you say that?' Roberts tried to make the question sound casual.

Butterfield hesitated; she was acutely conscious that the wrong word in the wrong place could cause all sorts of trouble for her, especially given the prospect of an official complaint about her conduct being submitted to the chief constable by Henry Masterson. However, the uneasy feeling had been growing, strengthened by Bill Harding's comment. Despite Alistair Marshall's argument that it was best to keep her thoughts to herself, Butterfield knew that was not possible. Yet, still she hesitated.

'Come on, love, spit it out,' said Roberts.

'It's just that none of this fits together, ma'am,' said Butterfield. 'And where are the DCI and Matty Gallagher? They've been missing for hours.'

Smart girl, thought Roberts. If Alison Butterfield could only learn to improve the way that she dealt with people, she had the makings of a fine detective.

'And why would Bill Harding threaten me when we were arresting Guthrie?' continued Butterfield.

'Bill Harding threatened you?' Roberts looked surprised. 'Are you sure?'

'He said that I would do well to remember than Henry Masterson has some influential friends.'

'He's probably sick of people pointing the finger at the estate over the shooting. He's already complained about you, remember.'

'Yes, I know,' said Butterfield, 'but it was the way that he said it. I definitely felt that it was intended to stop me asking any more awkward questions.'

'And did you hear this?' asked Roberts, glancing at Marshall.

'I am afraid not, ma'am. I was busy with Pete Guthrie.' He looked at Butterfield and made up his mind on the issue. 'But, for what it's worth, I'm with Alison. *Is* there something we're not being told?'

Roberts thought for a few moments then nodded.

'Yes, there is,' she said.

Before leaving the station for his meeting, Harris had told her that information should only be shared on a 'need-to-know' basis but she sensed that the two young detectives needed to know before their enthusiasm for the job led to them unwittingly jeopardise the investigation. The detective inspector stood up and walked over to close the squad room door then returned to her seat, watched expectantly by the young officers.

'You'll find out soon enough,' said Roberts in a low voice. 'I'm not sure about the estate being involved in the murder but you are right, Alison, there *is* something you have not been told, yes. The DCI has called a briefing at seven tomorrow morning to bring everyone up to speed but, in the meantime, none of what I am about to tell you goes out of this room.'

She gave them a stern look.

'Do you understand?' she asked.

The young detectives nodded and Alison Butterfield's eyes gleamed; this was why she had joined the police.

Chapter nineteen

Gallagher and Harris arrived back at Levton Bridge Police Station shortly after 4:00pm. Having brushed past a couple of reporters loitering outside the building, the inspector spent a few minutes in Gillian Roberts' office as he caught up with developments then went back to his own room and gave the dogs their tea. When they had finished, he picked up the Land Rover from in front of the police station, loaded the dogs into the back and headed for Geoff Morden's rented house in Tenter Street on the edge of town.

On arrival in the Victorian terrace, the inspector sat in the vehicle and gathered his strength for a few moments. The effects of his long night on the moor with only snatched sleep were beginning to catch up with him and he had dozed only fitfully as Gallagher drove them back from the meeting at the hotel. Now, having sat in the Land Rover with his eyes closed for five minutes, the inspector turned to look into the back of the vehicle where his dogs were sitting, watching him expectantly.

'We'll have a walk after this,' he said. 'Promise.'

The inspector got out of the vehicle and knocked on the front door of number twenty-seven, which was opened by Linda Morden. He could see that she had been crying and memories of a happier person flashed into his mind, of more innocent times, memories of a giggling six-year-old with ponytails and an impish sense of fun. It was the only time that he met Geoff's daughter and it had happened when, during a spell of leave from the Army, he had visited Manchester to see Geoff Morden to try to patch up their fractured friendship. The meeting had not gone well, the wounds were too fresh, and, although they did not argue, Harris had left after an hour. It was the last time they met before Morden returned to live in Levton Bridge.

Linda ushered Harris into the house.

'Long time no see, Jack,' she said with a sad smile. 'It must be twenty years. That afternoon in the back garden. You pushed me on the swing.'

'I'm surprised you still remember it.' Harris held his hand close to the floor. 'You were only yae high.'

'Oh, I remember it.'

Harris was startled when she moved forward and gave him a hug, holding him tight as they stood in the dark and musty hallway.

'Thank you for coming,' she whispered. 'I'm glad it's you.'

'Yes, but I'm still a detective,' said Harris. He gently disengaged himself from her hold. 'And one with a job to do.'

'Of course,' she said, stepping back. She looked embarrassed. 'Of course. Sorry.'

'Don't worry about it.'

Five minutes later, they were sitting nursing mugs of tea in the sparsely furnished living room, one with precious little sense of Geoff Morden, no family pictures, nothing. Linda guessed what he was thinking.

'Dad regarded this as a crash pad,' she said. 'Somewhere to live while the house was being built.'

Harris nodded.

'I'm afraid I gave your Detective Inspector Roberts a hard time earlier,' continued Linda. 'Apologise for me, will you?'

'I'm sure she understands.'

'It's just that you were a good friend of Dad's and I feel happier talking to you. He was so pleased that you had started seeing each other again.' Linda started crying. 'He was looking forward to the two of you walking the hills again. He said it would be like the old days.'

'Yeah, so was I.' Harris took a sip of tea and reached for a biscuit, aware of a sudden dip in energy after a day in which he had eaten little.

She continued to sob quietly and the inspector waited patiently for her tears to subside.

'But, good friend or not,' he said eventually, 'this isn't going to be easy. Whoever does it, they *are* going to have to ask some very difficult questions. If only to discover if your dad's death was accidental or if someone did it deliberately.'

'But who would do such a terrible thing?'

'That's what we need to find out,' said Harris. 'Was anything bugging him? Something in his private life, maybe? Was he in a relationship?'

'I sort of got the impression that he'd met someone up here but I don't know for certain. He was very good that way, was Dad. He never talked about that sort of thing because he knew it upset me because it brought back memories of Mum.'

'Did he mention a name?'

'Sorry. Like I said, it was only a feeling and he changed the subject when I asked him about it.'

'Is there anyone you can think of who might have wanted to harm your dad?' asked Harris. 'Someone he fell out with, perhaps?'

'No one,' said Linda.

'No one?'

'Look, I'm not stupid, Jack. I know that Dad wasn't an angel. He could rub people up the wrong way and he was always boasting about how much money he had earned – and some of his friends were a bit iffy but…'

'What do you mean iffy?' asked Harris.

'Well, Dad was still in touch with some of the bad lads from the old days,' said Linda. 'I know you don't talk to them because of the job but Dad did. He said that they were still friends, when all was said and done.'

'He never mentioned it.'

'He said that he didn't know how you would react. You being a police officer. But I don't want you to think that Dad had been dragged back into crime. He had put all that behind him.'

Harris did not reply but the more he learned about his old friend, the more he doubted the veracity of her statement. In Harris's view, Geoff Morden had not moved on at all from those reckless teenage years in the valley and the inspector was assailed by a sense of time standing still. With an effort, he dragged his mind back to the present day and the need to extract information without raising her suspicions.

'So, what had these lads done?' he asked. He tried to sound casual about it. Like it didn't really matter. He still did not know how much, if anything, she knew about the trafficking. 'Do you know?'

Linda hesitated.

'Come on, you've said it now,' said Harris.

'Dad said it was drugs.'

'Did he mention any names, by any chance?'

'I'd rather not say,' said Linda.

'This *is* a murder inquiry, you know.'

'You think I don't know that?' The tears welled up again.

'I'm sorry,' said Harris. 'That was insensitive but it would help to know what kind of people he was dealing with.'

'I know, but they don't sound like pleasant people and the last thing I want is any of them thinking that I have been passing on information about them.'

'Don't worry, this will be between you and me,' said Harris. 'The names?'

'Stuart Davis. He's mentioned a man called Stuart Davis a few times recently.'

'Now there's a blast from the past,' murmured Harris. 'I haven't thought of him in years. I'd completely lost track of him, in fact.'

'So had Dad, then he got in touch last year. He'd been living in Spain but he'd come back. They talked on the phone occasionally and met up for a drink a couple of times.'

'When was this?'

'The last time was three or four months ago. Dad went to Manchester for the night to see him. Look, I don't want you to think that Dad approved of what Stuart was doing.'

Harris nodded; his instincts told him that it was time to back off. If he pushed it too far at this stage, he could ruin everything and the last thing he wanted to do was attract the derision of a Ged Rutherford desperate to regain face after the security breach.

'I'm sure you're right,' said Harris. He gave her a reassuring look. 'Geoff was a law-abiding man, I know that, and I can't see that him having a few drinks with an old friend is that significant, to be honest. Best I know these things, though. Tell me, did your father ever mention a man called Bill Harding?'

'No. Who's he?'

'He works for the Hewby Moor Estate.'

'So, you still think that Dad was killed over the birds?' she asked.

'It's still a possibility.' Harris lowered his voice to make it sound like he was taking her into his confidence. 'Let me level with you, Linda. Emotions have been running pretty hot up here and when that happens in a close community like this, the results can be disastrous. The estate is our main focus at the moment, yes, but I'd appreciate it if you could not tell anyone at this stage.'

'Of course, I won't. Are you planning to arrest this fellow Harding?'

'We're not quite there yet but we're close.' Harris glanced up at the wall clock, drained his mug of tea and stood up. 'I'm sorry, Linda, but I have to go. I have someone else to see. What are your plans now?'

'I'm going to take Dad's things back to Manchester tomorrow. Gary and one of the lads are coming up in a van. They'll be here about nine-thirty.'

'Gary?'

'Gary Nesbitt,' she said. 'Our finance director.'

Harris headed for the door and walked into the hallway.

'I need to organise the funeral,' said Linda as he opened the front door and stepped out into the street. 'Is that alright?'

'Yes, that's fine.'

'Thanks for coming,' she said as he stepped down onto the pavement. Her eyes glistened with tears. 'Dad always said that you were alright for a copper.'

'You take care,' said Harris.

* * *

Once back in the Land Rover, the inspector sat deep in thought for a couple of moments then made a call on his mobile.

'Matty,' he said, 'you got anyone available to do a little job for me?'

'Alison's free.'

'No, not her. See, I need someone to go back to Hewby Moor and her presence would only inflame things given the day they've had.'

'What about Sally then?' said Gallagher.

'Ideal. Henry won't be so suspicious if we send our youngest officer.'

'What's the job?'

Having outlined his request, Harris made another call.

'Well if it isn't 007,' said Graham Leckie. 'I was going to ring you. Don't appreciate you holding out on us, old son. No one does. Ged's spitting bullets. Reckons you made him look stupid, and Jenny's not impressed either. Bunch of flowers time.'

'I had no option, Graham. You know what MI5 are like. I hope that you and I are not going to fall out over this.'

'Of course, we won't,' said Leckie. 'I already know that you're a twat.'

Harris smiled. Graham Leckie was one of the inspector's few close friends, the two men having met when Harris worked in Manchester and bonded over their shared love of wildlife. Even though Harris eventually returned home to Levton Bridge, they still talked on a regular basis because Leckie's work in force intelligence meant that he often had useful information on criminals heading north to commit crime in the valley.

'Anyway,' said Leckie. 'What can I do for you now that you have deigned to talk to us mere mortals?'

'I might be able to make amends. I want to run a name past you.'

'Go on.'

'A blast from my tearaway past.' Harris's mind went back once more to his teenage years in the valley. He recalled one incident in particular, when Stuart Davis, high on weed, set fire to garden sheds in the allotments in Levton Bridge while the watching Harris realised that the time had come to leave the area he loved. 'A guy called Stuart Davis. He used to deal in drugs, cannabis when I knew him, but I lost track of him.'

'Why so interested?'

'I've just found out that he had been talking to Geoff.'

'Where's this come from?' asked Leckie.

'Geoff's daughter. I've just been with her.'

'Do you think she knows about the guns?' asked Leckie.

'If she does, it was a damned good act, Graham. She comes over as a bit naïve, actually. She thinks her dad had put his dodgy past behind him.'

'The evidence would seem to suggest otherwise.'

Harris waited for the usual sound of Leckie tapping on his keyboard as he called up his database but heard nothing.

'You going to check him?' asked the inspector eventually.

'I don't need to check the file on Stuart Davis, matey. I know all about him. He's still a drug dealer.'

'Still active?'

'Yeah. He'd been abroad, that's why you lost track of him. Fled to Spain because police were getting too close.' Now came the sound of the tapping on the keyboard. 'Looks like he left the UK in 2001 but he turned up a year and a half ago and started working for Lynton Jago. He's been handling Jago's business in Liverpool for the past year and a half.'

'Drugs, I assume?'

'Yeah, Jago hooked up with one of the Scouse mobs to push cocaine into Manchester. It's why Ged's so interested in him. What we didn't know until George Matthews started talking was that Jago had a link with Geoff Morden. It could explain why we were struggling to track down the drugs shipments, if they've been smuggling the gear hidden away in his trucks. Mind if I tell Ged about this?'

'Be my guest.'

Harris ended the call, sat and thought for a few moments before reaching for the Land Rover's ignition.

'Stuart Davis,' he murmured. Memories of a tousle-headed teenager came to mind, a man with a scant regard for the law and a lopsided grin which could so easily be banished by a fearsome temper that could flare up at any moment. Harris shook his head. 'Some people never learn.'

He was about to turn on the engine when the ringing of his phone banished thoughts of the old days. It was Jenny. He sighed and took the call. No point in putting it off.

'I know, I know,' he said before she could speak. 'I'm a bastard and you're too good for me.'

'So long as you realise it,' she said. 'Carnations. Pink ones. And a nice bunch, not some scuddy end-of-line stuff from a petrol station.'

'What?'

'The bunch of flowers Leckie told you to buy me.'

'The man is insufferable,' said Harris. The words were uttered affectionately, though. 'Did you just ring up to make me feel bad?'

'No.' She lowered her voice, suddenly serious. 'Ged's paranoid about letting any of his team stay with George Matthews until he knows who's leaking the information, so he has asked me to do it. That OK?'

'Yeah, sure. You got a time yet?'

'Not yet. Tonight.'

Harris ended the call, stared at the phone, daring it to ring, then turned to the dogs in the rear of the Land Rover.

'We'll just go and see Harry then have that walk,' he said. 'I promise.'

* * *

Ten minutes later, the inspector was sitting in the cosy kitchen of a terraced house on the other side of town with Harry Groves and his wife. Groves still looked pale.

'How are you bearing up, Harry?' asked Harris. He took a sip from his mug of tea; three sugars, he needed the energy.

'I'm OK.'

'I think young DC Orr came to take your statement?'

'Yes, she did. She was very kind.'

Groves' wife nodded.

'She was very sympathetic,' said Moira. 'Such a nice young girl.'

'And you haven't remembered anything else about what happened?' asked Harris, looking at Groves.

'Nothing, Jack, and I keep going over it time and time again in my mind.'

'You told DC Orr that he'd been a bit distracted,' said Harris.

'Yes, I assumed that it was about the birds.'

'Could it have been something to do with a relationship?' asked the inspector. 'Someone he's started seeing up here, maybe? Do you know anything about that?'

'I am afraid not,' said Harry. He glanced at Moira but she said nothing. 'No, I assumed it was everything that was going on with the birds. He wasn't comfortable with the way Pete Guthrie was shouting his mouth off and splitting apart the club, and he didn't like the way he swore at Bill Harding's family at The Hillview either. Pete seems sure that Henry Masterson had something to do with what happened to Geoff.'

'Yeah, but he hasn't given us a single shred of evidence.' Harris stood up, drained his mug of tea and headed for the door. 'Anyway, let me know if you remember anything else, will you?'

'Sure, Jack.'

* * *

Once back in the Land Rover, Harris headed out of town and parked in a lay-by alongside the main valley road where he took the dogs out. For the next hour, they ranged across the hillside, the inspector's energy levels rising all the time as the landscape worked its customary magic on him, particularly when he lifted his binoculars to his eyes and watched a female buzzard as it quartered the sun-dappled slopes in search of prey.

Halfway round their route, they stopped at a rocky outcrop and Harris sat down and closed his eyes as the evening sun warmed his face. After a few moments, his thoughts drifted back to the forest clearing in Kosovo, as they had done on so many occasions in recent months. As usually happened on such occasions, the image of the dead children loomed large in his mind. Never a man with much empathy for children, the inspector's burgeoning relationship with Jenny Armannsson had prompted him to consider, for the first time, the thought that one day he might have a family of his own. That he may become a father. That he may introduce children to an evil world.

The counsellor had warned him during their sessions that such thoughts might prove troubling and that the doubts would always be there – it was, she said, part of the parenthood experience and something he would have to learn to live with. She had helped him find ways to focus on more positive thoughts when the darkness descended and he did so now, opened his eyes, drank in the sun-dappled hillside scenery and recalled happier times. This time, however, the thoughts only led him back to two teenagers roaming the hills before more difficult times tore apart their friendship and to the tears of a daughter for her murdered father many years later.

Harris sighed, stood up and he and the dogs continued their walk back to the Land Rover. Harris was loading the dogs into the back of the vehicle, when his mobile phone rang.

'Thought it was too good to last,' he said.

He leaned against the vehicle to take the call.

'Jenny,' he said. 'Any news?'

'Ged thinks that our police station is still being watched so we're going to have to box clever to get our VIPs out of the city. If everything goes to plan, we should be with you by eleven, eleven-thirty. That OK?'

'Fine.'

'Where can we make the switch?' she asked.

'I'll text you a GPS location.'

Harris ended the call, got into the vehicle and glanced back at the dogs.

'Eleven-thirty,' he said. 'Who needs sleep anyway?'

* * *

'And Jack Harris sent you, did he?' asked Henry Masterson.

It was just past 7:00pm and he looked suspiciously at Sally Orr, who had just arrived at the front door of his house on the Hewby Moor Estate.

'Yes, but it's nothing to worry about,' said the detective constable brightly. 'Something Alison Butterfield forgot to do earlier. Purely routine.'

'What's purely routine?'

'DCI Harris wants to see your bookings for grouse shooting days over the past couple of years.'

'And why would he want that?' asked Masterson.

'Like I said, it's just routine. Dotting the Is and crossing the Ts, he said.'

'Well, I'm not sure that I want to–'

'I'll get in trouble if I don't get them.'

Masterson looked at her worried expression for a few moments. Either he was getting older or she was very young. Where on earth did they get them from? he wondered.

'Well, anything to help, I suppose,' he said reluctantly. 'You'll have to come over to the office, mind.'

Five minutes later, the detective constable was sitting at a desk with a printed list in front of her.

'If you tell me what you're looking for–' began Masterson.

'Nothing in particular.' Orr ran a finger down the list of names and stopped three quarters of the way down the page. 'I wonder, would you be able to do me a photocopy, please?'

'If you insist but I don't see what use–'

'That's very kind of you,' said Orr.

The constable watched as he printed the copy then she headed for the door.

'I'm sorry to have troubled you,' she said. 'Thank you for your help.'

She walked out into the yard and Masterson stood and watched her as she got into her car. He looked down the list with a thoughtful expression on his face and his gaze came to a halt on one name in particular.

'Now, what's your game, Jack?' he murmured.

Chapter twenty

Lynton Jago was sitting in his office just after 7:00pm, with his eyes closed and his brow furrowed with pain. His headache had returned as the lack of sleep finally caught up with him and the ibuprofen was having little effect. There was a knock on the door and Stuart Davis walked in. Jago opened his eyes and looked balefully at his nervous expression.

'You'd better not be bringing me any more bad news,' he said.

'It's about the shipment.' Davis hesitated. 'Looks like we're going to have to take the delivery tomorrow after all.'

Jago sat forward and glared at him.

'I told you to postpone it,' he said. 'There's too many eyes on us. I told you that.'

'Yeah, and I told our friends in Hertfordshire that but they think differently.'

'What do you mean, think differently?' growled Jago. 'Who the fuck do they think they're dealing with?'

'They've set a date for their first attack,' said Davis. 'Four days from now. A city centre railway station somewhere in the North. They wouldn't tell me where.

They said I should watch out for it on the news. They need the shipment to come over now.'

'And are the Kosovans OK with that?'

'Yeah, they are,' said Davis. 'They're all ready to go. It means they get their money quicker, doesn't it?'

'And Gary Nesbitt?' asked Jago. 'What does he think about it?'

'He's OK with it, too. His driver is over there at the moment. They're just waiting for the word from you.'

'And we're sure that the police aren't onto any of this?' asked Jago.

'How many drug runs have we done with Speedwagonz now – six, seven? – and there's never been any bother, has there? The cops have no idea. Trust me, it'll be fine.'

'Yeah, well, I've got a bad feeling about this,' said Jago. 'And I don't like the idea of Jack Harris sniffing around.'

'He's no bother. I've just come off the phone from Gary. Harris told Linda that they still think Geoff was shot because of the birds. They're not far off making an arrest. Some bloke that works for the estate.'

'And Rutherford?'

'He's too busy trying to hide George Matthews away to think about anything else,' said Davis.

'You found out where Matthews is yet?' asked Jago. 'I'd like to get my money back.'

'Our girl reckons that Rutherford may move him somewhere out of town tonight. She's trying to find out where. What about it then? Do we go ahead with the firearms run?'

Jago thought for a few moments then nodded.

'Yes,' he said. 'But against my better judgement.'

Davis looked relieved and headed for the door.

'You'd better be right, though,' said Jago as he disappeared into the corridor. 'And keep looking for Matthews. I want him silenced.'

As Jago sat and listened to the clump of Davis's shoes on the stairs, the gang boss could not shake the feeling that he had just made a terrible mistake. A memory muscled its way to the forefront of his thoughts and, sitting in the chill of his office, he remembered the final visit of the only police officer he had ever feared. Jago could handle Ged Rutherford and his ilk but there had always been something different about Jack Harris. A sense that the detective was prepared to step the wrong side of the line to get what he wanted. Jago recalled once more the way the inspector had stood in the office, spitting out his parting words through gritted teeth: 'I'll get you. So help me, Lynton, one day I'll get you.'

Now, as then, Jago felt his blood run cold as the doubts crowded in on him. He toyed with calling Davis back and asserting himself, ordering that the firearms stay in Kosovo until the heat was off and that they only moved when he, and no one else, gave the order to move them. Jago shook his head and winced at the stabbing pain. No, he thought, he could not afford to cancel the run at this late hour. Lynton Jago had built his reputation on delivering what he had promised and any sign of weakness now would be disastrous for his reputation. There were plenty of younger people ready to step into his shoes should he slip up – he knew that only too well. No, he decided, the game would have to play out.

* * *

Jack Harris had several hours to kill before George Matthews and his wife were delivered into his care so he took the opportunity to go home to his remote cottage, which stood halfway up a hillside on the valley road several miles from Levton Bridge and was accessed by a steep and winding rocky path. Harris had renovated the property himself in the year following his return to the area, having stumbled across it while out walking. For the inspector, the big attraction of the cottage was that he could not see any other properties when he stood on the front doorstep.

After giving the dogs their supper, he grabbed a shower, glad to get out of the clothes he had been wearing for the best part of two days, then microwaved himself a ready meal. He was dozing in his favourite armchair in the living room when his phone rang. Temporarily disorientated, the inspector groaned, struggled to work out where he was, then snapped out a hand to the side table and grasped the device.

'Susan,' he said.

'We've just heard from our informant,' said Peters. She sounded excited. 'The firearms are on their way out of Kosovo.'

Harris sat up, now wide awake.

'Already?' he said. 'I thought you reckoned we might have a day or two.'

'It appears that the group have brought their plans forward for the attack. I told you they were serious.'

'I never doubted it,' said Harris. 'Do you know where they plan to do it?'

'Our informant thinks it's something to do with a railway station. Our techies have finally managed to access the mobile used by one of the ringleaders so we should get more information soon.'

'Do we know which lorry the guns are on?' asked Harris.

'We do, yes. It's due to arrive in Dover tomorrow then stop off somewhere en route to offload the guns.'

'Do you know where?'

'Our informant does not know for certain but we're thinking that it's most likely to be the Speedwagonz depot in Manchester. If it is there, Ged's people will handle it.'

'And where do I fit into things?' asked Harris.

A pause.

'You don't,' she said eventually.

'But I've been more heavily involved than Ged has.'

'I know but the decision's taken. Wherever it happens, the locals will handle it and, if that means Manchester, it's down to Ged to organise – and he's adamant that you won't be involved. Politics, I'm sure you understand.'

'Only too well,' said Harris darkly.

'Oh, don't throw a moody on me, Jack. Think what you would do if the truck offloaded the guns in your area and another force tried to muscle in.'

Harris considered the comment for a few moments.

'It's a fair point, I suppose,' he said grudgingly.

'You know it – and, if it makes you feel any better, it should lead to Lynton Jago finally being arrested.'

'I always rather hoped it might be me who lifted him.' The inspector had moved into the kitchen and switched on the kettle. 'Mind, we're still not a hundred per cent certain if he's involved, are we?'

'We are now. Our techies have also identified a mobile phone used by Gary Nesbitt at Speedwagonz – one we did not know he owned – and it turns out that he's been in regular contact with Stuart Davis. Three times in the past twelve hours. Looks like our Mister Nesbitt is in this up to his neck along with Jago.'

'And Linda? Where does she fit into things?'

'Not sure.'

'Maybe her father was killed because he wouldn't go through with it,' said Harris. He dropped a teabag into a mug. 'I don't imagine that a lifelong Labour voter was overjoyed at delivering guns to a bunch of fascists. Perhaps he was one of the good guys, after all.'

'Don't get your hopes up, Jack. Once a bad 'un, always a bad 'un.'

'Speak for yourself,' said Harris.

Chapter twenty-one

It was shortly before midnight when the two black cars with tinted windows drove slowly into the car park next to the hilltop viewing area ten miles from Levton Bridge. Waiting in another unmarked car were Jack Harris and Matty Gallagher and, parked behind them, a second vehicle contained two armed officers, one of them Davy Morrison. The black cars pulled to a halt and Gerry Bayliss got out of the driver's seat of one of them, followed from the passenger's side by Jenny Armannsson. Bayliss was wearing a sidearm and both of them looked uneasy. Harris and Gallagher got out of their own car and the inspector nodded a welcome to Bayliss.

'Gerry,' he said. 'Long time no see.'

The men shook hands and Armannsson resisted the urge to give Harris a quick kiss; she'd learnt her lesson in the hotel room earlier in the day. Or rather had re-learned it. She had always known that Jack Harris was not a man to mix business with pleasure. As Morrison and his armed colleague took up positions at the entrance to the car park, Bayliss peered out at the darkened hills, which were only vaguely visible beyond the arc of the headlights.

'Couldn't you get anywhere more remote?' he asked. 'Even the bloody satnav shut up in the end.'

'We do our best,' said Harris. 'You got our VIPs then?'

Bayliss nodded towards one of the black cars.

'In the back,' he said. 'Be warned, Esther is spitting bullets.'

'As long as she's the only one,' said Harris. 'Are you sure that you weren't followed?'

'We took that many back streets in Manchester even I didn't know where I was,' said Bayliss. 'If Jago did have a tail on us, we lost him a long way back. There was certainly nothing on the M6. Where are you going to keep George and his missus?'

'You know better than that, Gerry.'

Bayliss nodded.

'Need-to-know,' he said. 'And I don't need to know. Frankly, I don't want to know. Be warned, Jago is panicking. He's pulling out all the stops to track down Matthews.'

'Are we going to do this then?' said Harris. 'We don't want to draw attention to ourselves.'

Bayliss peered into the darkness again.

'What, up here?' he said.

'You'd be surprised,' said Harris. 'This place is Poacher Central on a nice night like this.'

Bayliss glanced back to one of the black cars and gave a thumbs up. Two armed officers emerged from the vehicle and opened the back doors to allow a nervous-looking George Matthews to emerge, accompanied by a small woman who looked like her lips had been welded shut. Esther peered into the darkness and gave her husband a look of disapproval.

'You're right,' said Gallagher, looking at Bayliss, 'our George is definitely not exactly flavour of the month, is he?'

'Thank God I was driving the other car,' said Bayliss. 'Apparently, she was giving him pelters all the way up here. Turns out she'd always wanted to go to Acapulco.'

He grinned and Gallagher laughed. Harris walked over to the couple.

'I am DCI Jack Harris,' he said. 'I'll be responsible for your safety while you're staying in this area.'

'I've heard of you,' said George Matthews.

'Not all of it bad, I hope, Mr Matthews.'

Matthews did not reply.

'Where are you taking us?' demanded Esther.

Harris said nothing and looked at Bayliss.

'OK, Gerry,' he said, 'you've done your job. We'll take it from here. Best you get away.'

'My pleasure,' said Bayliss. He looked at Matthews. 'Good luck, George.'

Within a minute, the black cars had left the car park and were heading off down the valley and into the night.

'*Were* you followed?' said Harris, watching them go, then turning to Armannsson.

'I don't think so, Jack. We've pretty much had the road to ourselves, like Gerry said.'

'Right.'

'Don't you trust him?'

'I don't trust anyone.' Harris gestured to the Matthewses. 'Come on, let's get you somewhere safe.'

* * *

Twenty minutes later, the two cars pulled off the main valley road and made their way with dipped headlights up a rough hillside track until they reached a small white cottage.

'Home, sweet home,' said Harris. He brought the car to a halt and glanced round at the Matthewses in the back seat. 'Once the firearms boys have checked it out, we can go in.'

It did not take the officers long to complete their checks and Morrison soon appeared at the front door and gave a thumbs up. Harris and Gallagher led the couple into the house, followed by Armannsson. Esther Matthews wrinkled her nose at the musty smell as she stepped into the hallway.

'When was the last time someone lived here?' she sniffed.

'Not for the best part of a year,' said Harris. 'It's a holiday let but it needs repairs so they've not had anyone in for a long time.'

'Certainly not a cleaner,' said Esther.

She ran a finger disapprovingly across a dusty side table as Harris led the couple into the living room and moved to the window, where he watched as the armed officers took a couple of overnight bags from the boot of their car and carried them into the cottage. Harris drew the curtains and turned back into the room.

'Are you sure we will be safe here?' asked George.

'You should be, yes,' replied Harris.

'That's what DCI Rutherford said.'

'Well, I'm not him.' Harris walked over to the fireplace, knelt down and reached for the pile of newspapers. 'I told the letting agent that you are a couple of friends out to do some birdwatching. I said you would only be staying a few days and didn't want to be disturbed.'

'Is this our life now?' asked Esther. She sat down heavily on one of the threadbare armchairs. 'Being moved from crappy place to crappy place?'

'It'll feel better when we get a fire going,' said Harris. 'But the main thing is that very few people know that this place is even here, including Lynton Jago and his goons. As to what happens in the longer term, that's down to Ged Rutherford.'

Esther glared at her husband, who was standing in the middle of the room, as if unsure what to do next.

'I hope you're proud of what you have done,' she said.

'What your husband has done,' said Harris, turning round with a log in his hand, 'is something very brave. Lynton Jago has ruined an awful lot of lives down the years and, if George's evidence can help us put him behind bars, he'll have done society a massive favour.'

'What my husband has done,' said Esther with venom, 'is steal a million pounds and try to jet off to Acapulco without his wife. What my husband has done is prove what a bastard he is.'

'I guess you are going to have to sort that out between yourselves,' said Harris. He returned to making the fire, then looked up at Morrison, who had emerged from the kitchen. 'Happy?'

'Delirious,' said Morrison. 'At least your lot have stocked the fridge up. Bacon and eggs for breakfast.'

The second firearms officer walked into the room from the hallway, cradling his weapon in his arms.

'All quiet out there?' asked Harris.

'As the grave.'

Esther gave a slight sob.

'Sorry,' said the firearms officer. 'Poor turn of phrase.'

Gallagher, who was sitting on one of the other armchairs, gave a low laugh. Harris lit the fire and stared at it for a few moments before giving a grunt of satisfaction when he was content that the flames had caught hold. He straightened up and looked at George Matthews.

'Tell me something,' he said. 'What on earth made you think that you could steal from Lynton Jago and get away with it? You must have known what the man was like?'

'Madness,' said Matthews. 'Sheer madness.'

Esther snorted her derision.

'Greed, more like,' she said. 'You're a silly old fool, George. What on earth did you think you were going to do in Acapulco anyway? You get sunburned in Blackpool.'

Harris glanced at Gallagher and gave him a wry smile.

'Time to go, I think,' he said.

Gallagher nodded and stood up.

'I reckon so,' he said. 'I could certainly do with some kip.'

Harris looked at Armannsson.

'You going to be OK?' he asked.

'Ask me in the morning,' she said.

* * *

A weary Lynton Jago had returned to his detached mock-Elizabethan house on the edge of Manchester shortly before 10:30pm and, after a couple of glasses of whisky, had fallen asleep in his armchair in front of the television. It proved to be a troubled sleep as he dreamt about Jack Harris turning up to arrest him at his daughter' s wedding on a Caribbean beach. The dream was disturbed by the insistent ringing of his smartphone. Jago groaned, spent a couple of moments trying to work out where he was and reached for it on a side table. He glanced at the wall clock – one o'clock – and lifted his mobile to his ear.

'Do you know what fucking time it is?' he said.

'Yeah, sorry about that,' said Stuart Davis. 'But I thought you'd like to know that our girl was right. Matthews and his wife *have* been taken out of Manchester.'

'Do we know where?' Jago was wide awake now.

Davis hesitated.

'Well?' said Jago.

'She thinks that Jack Harris has got them,' said Davis eventually.

'Why the fuck has Jack Harris got them?'

'Rutherford thought that it would be difficult for us to find them in the hills, apparently.'

'Do we know exactly where they are being held?' asked Jago.

'She doesn't know. Somewhere pretty remote, she thinks.'

'Well, she'd better find out.'

'I'm not sure she can,' said Davis. 'She's done well to find out that much, as it is. Rutherford is leaning on everybody and, if she starts asking too many questions, he'll know it's her who's been leaking information.'

'Well, what about your mate?' asked Jago. 'He lives there. Can't he find out where they are?'

'I'm just about to ring him,' said Davis. 'If anyone can find him, he can. He knows those hills like the back of his hand.'

'Well, you just make sure he does,' growled Jago.

He ended the call, replaced the phone on the table and sighed as a stab of pain signalled the return of his headache. It was a headache he recognised from the days when Jack Harris and his team were smashing down doors in Manchester.

* * *

Having rumbled its way through the darkness on largely empty roads, the Speedwagonz truck passed across the Hungarian border and entered Austria with its deadly cargo concealed amid a large number of boxes containing tinned fruit.

Chapter twenty-two

Jack Harris stood at the front of the briefing room at Levton Bridge Police Station and surveyed the small number of officers who had gathered, with a grave expression on his face. It was shortly before 7:00am and the group included Roberts and Gallagher, who were sitting in the front row, and Butterfield, Marshall and Sally Orr on the chairs ranged behind them. Orr's eyes gleamed as she drank in every detail of her first major CID briefing and contemplated the role that she was to play. Butterfield smiled at her; it was not long since she had been the excited newbie. Several other officers were in the room as well, including the divisional commander Philip Curtis. All eyed the DCI expectantly as he spoke; what they were hearing excited them.

'I don't need to remind you that what you are being told here is strictly confidential,' said Harris solemnly. 'MI5 operations demand the utmost secrecy and anyone who breathes a word outside this room will immediately be suspended pending a full disciplinary hearing. Lives are at stake here and I don't want anyone at Levton Bridge blamed for messing things up. Isn't that right, sir?'

Curtis nodded; he was relishing being at the heart of something big. Reputations could be made and lost on the turn of such events and the commander was pleased to see that Harris's words had had the desired effect and that the atmosphere in the room had grown heavy with tension as the extent of the investigation was outlined. Harris turned back to the noticeboard behind him, on which were pinned a number of photographs.

'And I suggest that you memorise these faces,' he said, 'because the pictures will be taken down when we are finished.'

Harris tapped an image of Geoff Morden, which had been taken in the mortuary at Roxham General Hospital during Doc's post-mortem the previous day.

'Despite all the things that are going on,' said the inspector, 'our primary task remains the same – to find out who killed Geoff Morden and why they did it.'

'Surely it's clear?' said Gallagher. 'He was a villain who thought that providing guns to far-right activists was a step too far and said the wrong thing to the wrong person.'

'If so, it's likely that he said it to this man.' Harris pointed to a grainy image taken from a surveillance picture supplied by Leckie. 'Lynton Jago. Manchester Organised Crime think he has been using Speedwagonz trucks to smuggle cocaine so he would easily be able to accommodate a consignment of firearms. What's more, Lynton Jago doesn't do scruples, so he would not care who they went to so long as he was paid.'

Harris turned back to the noticeboard and tapped a police image of a lean-faced young man.

'And neither would he,' he said. 'This is a very old mug shot of Stuart Davis. Taken the last time he was arrested in the UK, back in 2000, not long after which he fled to Spain. He's been Lynton Jago's Mr Fixit since returning a year or so ago.'

'And he's a nasty piece of work,' said Gillian Roberts. 'I knew him when he was a teenager up here and it doesn't sound like he's changed much. I'm not surprised he's tied up with far-right types either – he was an out and out racist, was Stuart.'

'Indeed, he was,' said Harris. 'He was also an old friend of Geoff Morden's and there is every reason to believe that Geoff became involved in the drug trafficking because Davis suggested it. In my view, Stuart Davis is perfectly capable of organising Geoff Morden's murder if Jago asked him to.'

Harris gave them all another grave look.

'However, Geoff Morden was not the only potential threat to Jago,' he said. 'You also need to know that we are looking after a witness whose safety has been compromised. Suffice to say that Jago would dearly like him silenced. Another reason to keep these proceedings confidential, ladies and gentlemen. We are swimming in murky waters.'

A low murmur of excitement ran round the room. Harris waited for it to die out; he was enjoying the impact that his briefing was having. When the room had fallen silent again, he turned back to the board and tapped another picture, this time an image that had been photocopied from a newspaper cutting. The murmurs started up again.

'There's someone else we should not forget in all of this,' said Harris after they had died away once more. 'You all know Henry Masterson, I think.'

'But surely we know that this isn't about the birds?' protested Philip Curtis. 'We're only saying it is to prevent Jago suspecting that we know about the firearms. There's nothing to point to Henry. That theory went out of the window the moment that we discovered that Geoff Morden was involved with Jago.'

'I'd have said the same thing until Bill Harding threatened Alison,' replied Harris. 'That's not the action of an innocent man and Bill doesn't sneeze without Henry's say-so.'

'But isn't it more likely that she just misinterpreted what he said?' Curtis looked at Butterfield. 'No offence, Alison, but threatening people is just not Bill's style.'

'I know what I heard, sir.'

'And that's good enough for me,' said Harris.

Butterfield shot him a grateful look and the inspector gave her the merest of winks.

'Go on then,' said Curtis. 'Convince me.'

Harris looked at Sally Orr, who was sitting clutching the photocopy she had obtained the previous evening.

'Show him, Constable,' he said.

Orr held up the sheet of paper.

'Bill Harding was right when he told Alison that Henry Masterson has some influential friends,' she said.

'You see,' said Harris, looking back at the picture of Masterson on the board, 'there had been rumours that a group of gangland figures from Merseyside came up to the Hewby Moor Estate for a shooting weekend last year. I put it down to local gossip at the time. Henry's not the most popular of men and there's plenty who will stir up trouble for him. We've seen that with Pete Guthrie. That was my mistake. I should have listened to Matty.'

Gallagher nodded his appreciation at the comment.

'It was only when I heard from Leckie that Stuart Davis was back in the UK and based in Liverpool that I really started thinking about it,' said Harris. 'However, all the credit must go to Matty. He flagged it up first.'

'Credit for what?' asked Curtis, not sure that he wanted to know the answer.

'For confirming Masterson's criminal connections,' said Gallagher. 'See, last night, we sent Sally to ask him for a list of people who have booked grouse shooting weekends in the past couple of years.'

'And I take it that the rumour was true, after all?' asked Curtis bleakly. His mind was already playing out the ramifications and none of them were encouraging.

'It certainly was.' Orr held up the piece of paper again. 'Stuart Davis was the one who made the booking.'

'But are we really saying that Henry Masterson is tied up with all this?' The commander looked at Harris. 'The man's a pillar of the community and I heard the other day that he's in line to be the next Lord Lieutenant. If you're wrong, he'll have us all issuing parking tickets for the rest of what remains of our careers.'

The commander switched his attention to Orr.

'And for some of our younger colleagues, that's an awful lot of tickets,' he said with the merest of smiles. 'Less so for us somewhat more mature officers, eh, Jack?'

Laughter ran round the room and Harris gave a nod of appreciation at the commander's attempt to defuse the tension. The last thing he wanted was a fight with the divisional commander.

'Unfortunately, yes,' said Harris. 'Look, sir, I don't know what I'm saying about Henry Masterson but I don't think we can afford to ignore it.'

Curtis nodded.

'Just be careful,' he said.

'Always,' said the inspector. He glanced at the wall clock. 'Right, ladies and gentlemen, time's getting on. To next steps. Are we any nearer to finding out if Geoff Morden had a girlfriend up here? It's a loose end and I don't like loose ends.'

Marshall shook his head.

'No one seems to know anything,' he said. 'I am beginning to doubt if she exists.'

'Keep looking.' Harris looked at Roberts. 'As the DI keeps quite rightly reminding me, most murders are committed by people close to the victim and I want to make sure that we're not missing anything.'

* * *

Ten minutes later, the briefing was over and the inspector was standing in one of the cells, looking at a chastened and dishevelled Pete Guthrie.

'Calmed down yet?' asked Harris.

Guthrie nodded.

'I was not thinking straight yesterday,' he said. 'I could easily have got myself shot like Geoff.'

'Look, Pete,' said Harris. He sat down next to him on the bench. 'If you know more than you are letting on about what happened, now really is the time to tell me.'

'I don't know much, Jack, but one thing I do know is that Geoff was frightened.' Guthrie's voice was quiet. The fury of the previous days had long since been banished.

'Frightened? Of what?'

'He never said anything but I could tell,' said Guthrie. 'I assumed that it was something to do with the birds and Masterson was the one that seemed most likely.'

'And why did you not tell me this before?'

'Would you have believed me?' Guthrie gave a wry smile. 'After all, like you always say, what evidence did I have? Just a vague feeling that I couldn't prove. And you had warned me that you'd charge me with breach of the peace if I kept saying things without anything to back it up. And you said that Masterson might sue me. I can't afford that, Jack. I can barely afford the mortgage, as it is.'

'Fair point.' Harris lowered his voice again. 'Look, Pete, you are going to have to trust me. There are things happening that you don't know about and, if I release you, I don't want to hear that you've tried to take things into your own hands again. I don't want my officers called to the estate again. Understand?'

Guthrie nodded and Harris stood up.

'I'll get the custody officer to let you go,' said the inspector. 'You may yet be charged but I've got bigger things to worry about at the moment.'

As Harris reached the door, he turned back to look at Guthrie.

'Did Geoff ever mention that he had a new woman in his life?' he asked. 'Someone up here, maybe?'

'I got the impression that there might have been someone but I don't know if there was. I did ask him one time but he laughed it off. Mind, he didn't really talk about things like that. Why, is it important?'

'Probably not,' said Harris. 'It's just nice to know these things.'

As the inspector walked out into the corridor, he was approached by a uniformed officer.

'Henry Masterson is in reception,' she said. 'With his lawyer. They want to see you.'

'Now there's a surprise,' said Harris.

Chapter twenty-three

Harris sat in the interview room next to the reception area at Levton Bridge Police Station and looked across the desk at a grim-faced Henry Masterson and a sallow besuited man. His solicitor. The atmosphere was tense.

'Level with me, Jack,' said Masterson. He leaned forward in his seat. 'Are me and Bill suspects?'

'What on earth makes you say that?'

'I hear things,' said Masterson.

'You know better than to listen to local tittle-tattle. You've always told me to ignore–'

'Oh, don't play games with me, man! I know you too well for that. There's that young constable who came round last night, for starters. Asking to see a list of people who had booked shooting weekends. Then there's Constable Butterfield's constant insinuations, which you have done nothing to prevent.'

'It feels,' said the lawyer, speaking for the first time in the meeting, 'as if my client is being harassed by the police.'

Harris did not reply.

'I don't want to make a big thing about this, Jack, I really don't,' said Masterson. He tried to sound more conciliatory. 'But people are talking. They hear things on the news and assume that I'm behind what happened. And from what I can see, you're happy to let it happen. I can't let that go on.'

'Just routine inquiries, Henry, that's all,' said Harris.

'If you tell me what Constable Orr was after last night, maybe I can help. I told you that I'd co-operate in any way I could.'

'Suffice to say that neither you nor Bill are suspects.'

'But you do think that it's possible Geoff Morden's death was something to do with the estate?'

'It's just one theory,' said Harris. 'Unless you have a better one, that is.'

'If you think it's something to do with Stuart Davis, you're barking up the wrong tree.'

'What makes you mention him?' asked Harris. He tried to sound casual but the alarm bells were ringing again.

'Because I know the way your devious mind works. Look, I'm not stupid. I know what Stuart is like but you can take it from me, he's got nothing to do with this. He just booked a weekend for some pals and I haven't heard from him since.' Masterson stood up. 'Anyway, I've said my piece. The next move is down to you, Jack, but be warned, I am prepared to take this further.'

As Masterson headed for the door, followed by the lawyer, Harris took one of the biggest gambles of his career. Backed his feeling that Henry Masterson could be trusted.

'Do me a favour, will you, Henry?' he said. 'Don't tell anyone about this conversation.'

'Why shouldn't I?' said Masterson, turning round. 'I've got my reputation to protect.'

'Just trust me, yeah? There are things happening.'

'What kind of things?'

'I can't say,' said Harris. 'Not yet anyway, but the wrong word to the wrong person could cause a lot of damage and put lives at risk.'

Masterson looked at the inspector's grave expression.

'Lives?' he said.

Harris nodded. Masterson thought for a few moments then nodded.

'OK,' he said. 'You've always been straight with me but I can't let this go on forever. It's not good for business having people think I go round shooting people.'

'I appreciate that.' Harris glanced at the wall clock and thought of the Speedwagonz truck rumbling its way across Europe towards Calais. 'Just give me twenty-four hours.'

Masterson glanced at his lawyer, who shrugged.

'Your call, Henry,' he said. 'It's your good name he's damaging.'

Masterson looked back at Harris and nodded.

'Twenty-four hours,' he said. 'But not a minute longer.'

And with that he and the lawyer were gone, leaving the inspector sitting at the desk and wondering if he'd just made a huge mistake. Shaking his head to banish the thought, he headed out of the interview room. On his way back to his office, Harris stopped in at the CID squad room. Sally Orr was the only officer present, hunched over her computer as she typed up notes. She stood hurriedly to her feet when Harris walked into the room but he motioned for her to sit down.

'I've just been with Henry Masterson,' said the inspector. He sat down at the desk opposite her. 'He didn't appreciate your visit last night. I suspect both you and Alison are off his Christmas card list.'

Orr looked anxious.

'What did he say?' she asked.

'That we are harassing him.'

'And what did you tell him?'

'To wind his head in,' said Harris. He gestured to her notes. 'Anything interesting?'

'I'm helping Alistair with his work to see if Geoff Morden had a girlfriend.'

'Anything?'

'Not really.'

Harris nodded and left the room. Seconds later, he was back.

'Oh, and well done,' he said. 'And don't worry about Henry. You didn't do anything wrong.'

'Thank you, sir.'

Orr could not contain the grin that overcame her as the inspector disappeared back into the corridor. It was like people always said, the man had a constant capacity to surprise. Harris was back in his office, sitting deep in thought as he sipped at a mug of tea, when his phone rang. He took the call.

'Susan,' he said. 'Any news on the truck?'

'It's in France. Should be in Dover later this afternoon. I've arranged for Customs to let it through. Listen, I'm ringing to see if you can help with something. Our techies say that Stuart Davis called a number last night and twice this morning. And he called it several times before that as well. We don't recognise the name, wondered if you do?'

'Who is it?' asked Harris.

After she had told him, the inspector was silent for a few moments.

'Are you sure it's his phone?' she said.

'I am, yes.' She read out the mobile number. 'Do I take it that you know him?'

Harris scrolled down the contact list on his smartphone to double-check the number before answering.

'I am afraid I do,' he said. 'Strike one to my DI.'

'What does that mean?'

'Always look close to home.'

He tensed as he looked at the name; it was the letting agent for the cottage where he had placed the Matthewses.

'Des,' said Harris. 'Everything OK?'

'Yeah, fine, Jack. I know you're busy but I'm getting in touch because Harry Groves has just been on. He's doing a ring-round because he's got some venison and wonders if anyone wants to take some? I know you said that your friends did not want to be disturbed but I told him I'd check if they wanted any of it. He's offered to take it up to the cottage, if they do.'

'That's very kind of you,' said Harris. He tried to sound calm. 'But it's fine. They're vegetarian.'

'OK, just thought I'd let you know.'

'It's appreciated, Des.'

When Harris had completed the call, he immediately rang Armannsson.

'Jenny,' he said, urgency in his voice, 'I have this awful feeling that we've been compromised. I'll be up within an hour but keep George Matthews away from the windows.'

'Why, what's happened?' The tone in his voice had scared her.

'I'll explain when I get there,' said Harris. 'But whatever you do, don't leave the cottage unless you have to.'

After finishing the call, the inspector walked quickly back to the CID room where Orr had just placed the desk phone back on its receiver and scribbled something on her notepad.

'Sally,' he said. 'I think I know who Geoff's girlfriend was.'

'So do I, sir. That was Alistair on the phone. He's tracked down a resident of Tenter Street who saw her leaving Geoff's house one night.' Orr held up the notepad so that the inspector could read it. 'Do we have the same name?'

Harris nodded.

'We do,' he said grimly. 'And if we're right, Geoff Morden's killer has been hiding in plain sight all the time.'

Chapter twenty-four

Jack Harris parked the Land Rover outside Geoff Morden's rented house in Tenter Street. Two men were coming out of the door carrying a table, one of them dressed in workman's overalls, the other in a cream shirt and smart black trousers. Harris watched them load the table into the back of a white van and walked over to address the smarter of the two.

'Gary Nesbitt?' he said.

'Yes, you must be Jack Harris.' The Speedwagonz financial director extended a hand in welcome. 'Linda's told me all about you. She's very grateful for your support. We both are.'

'Glad I can help,' said Harris.

Linda emerged from the house carrying a small box of books, and her face lit up when she saw Harris.

'Jack,' she said. She placed the box on the pavement and came over to give him a hug. This time, Harris did not resist. It was time to play the game.

'Any news?' she asked.

'Nothing concrete.' Harris looked at Nesbitt. 'Have you had any thoughts?'

Nesbitt shook his head.

'Nothing,' he said. 'Geoff was a businessman. There's no way anyone would want to kill him.'

'I'm inclined to agree with you,' said Harris. 'The more we think about it, the more we go back to our original theory that it was an accident. That whoever tried to kill the hen harriers killed Geoff instead.'

Gary Nesbitt nodded. Linda rubbed a hand across eyes that were glistening with tears.

'That's why I wanted to catch you before you went back,' said Harris. 'I didn't want you worrying that there might be someone out there with a grudge against yourselves.'

'We appreciate the gesture,' said Nesbitt. 'That puts our mind at rest, doesn't it, Lindy?'

She nodded.

'It does, yes,' she said. 'Do you think you'll be able to find out who it was, Jack? Is it this Bill Harding chap you mentioned?'

'We'll certainly be bringing him in for questioning, yes. Even if he wasn't the one who pulled the trigger, I reckon he knows who did.' The inspector gestured to the van, which was almost full. 'You look just about finished. You heading straight back to Manchester?'

'We have to drop the keys into the estate agent first,' said Linda. 'Then we'll be off.'

She glanced over as the man in the overalls put the box of books into the van.

'I have been dreading this moment,' she said. 'I know it sounds a strange thing to say but it's like confirmation that Dad's dead.'

'I understand,' said Harris.

Nesbitt put a comforting arm round her shoulders and looked at Harris.

'Is there anything we can do to help your investigation, Chief Inspector?' he asked.

'I don't think so,' said Harris. 'I'd appreciate it if you didn't tell anyone else about this conversation, though.'

'You can rely on us,' said Nesbitt.

The man in the overalls slammed shut the back door of the van and walked round to the driver's side.

'I'll let you get off,' said Harris. 'Look after yourself, Linda.'

'I will, Jack, and thank you again.' She gave him a light kiss on the cheek. 'Like I said, I'm glad it was you.'

Harris walked back to his vehicle and Linda looked at Gary.

'I'll just do a final check,' she said.

Nesbitt nodded, watched her enter the house, waited until Harris was back in the Land Rover then took his mobile phone out of his pocket and dialled a number.

'Stuart,' he said. 'It's Gary. Everything's OK. Harris is still convinced that Geoff's death is down to the birds. They're planning to bring somebody from the estate in for questioning.'

'Excellent,' said Davis. 'Where's the truck?'

'France. Should arrive tonight.'

'Let me know when,' said Davis. 'See you later.'

Nesbitt ended the call and clambered into the van from which he watched as Linda re-emerged from the house, locked the front door and walked over to the vehicle.

'Everything OK?' asked Nesbitt, shuffling over as she got into the vehicle.

'Yes, fine,' she said. 'Come on, let's drop these keys off and go home.'

'Good idea,' said Nesbitt.

As the van passed Harris in the Land Rover, Linda waved and the detective waved back. Seconds later, an anonymous blue car passed along the street and slotted in behind the van. Harris's phone rang.

'How long do you want us to follow them?' asked a man's voice.

'Until you hear different. GMP will pick them up further down the motorway, as planned.'

'Hokey-dokes.'

Harris replaced the phone in its cradle, started the Land Rover's engine and punched in another number.

'Wondered when you'd call,' said Rutherford. 'Jenny told me that your safe house has been compromised.'

'I suspect it has, yes,' said Harris. He edged the vehicle out into the road.

'Well, if it helps, the leak may be down to us. We think we've identified a girl in our Witness Protection Unit who's been passing information on to Stuart Davis. We'll pick her up when all this is over. Don't want to alert suspicions now.'

'I suspect this one is not down to her,' said Harris. 'No, I know exactly who it was.'

'You going to tell me?'

'Not until I'm sure, no. I've already slandered one perfectly innocent man this morning and I want to be certain.'

'Fair enough,' said Rutherford. 'Have you moved the Matthewses yet? I'd rather not take them back until I know exactly what the witness protection girl has told Davis.'

'I'm not planning to move them.'

There was silence from Rutherford for a few moments.

'You're not?' he said eventually.

'No. See, I've got this idea...'

* * *

Jack Harris went back to Levton Bridge Police Station to switch the Land Rover for an unmarked car then he and Gallagher headed out of town, bound for the safe house. The inspector was at the wheel as they left the built-up area behind and took the sunlit main valley road running between fields that were scattered with grazing sheep. There was silence in the vehicle for a few moments, broken, as ever, by the sergeant.

'Are you sure about this?' he said. 'What if the gunman slips through the net again... well, it's risky, isn't it?'

'We'll be waiting for him this time,' said Harris. 'And you can't approach the cottage without someone spotting you.'

'I hope you're right,' said Gallagher.

'So do I,' said Harris.

It took them half an hour to reach the cottage and, as the vehicle made its way up the rough track towards the property, the front door swung open and Jenny Armannsson stepped out. She watched their arrival with a tense expression on her face, constantly glancing across the nearby fields. Harris could see that Davy Morrison and his colleague were standing behind her in the hallway, their firearms at the ready. All three relaxed when they identified the new arrivals. The detectives got out of the vehicle and Harris let the dogs out of the back then reached down into the footwell to pick up a newspaper, before following Gallagher towards the cottage.

'Boy, am I glad to see you,' said Armannsson.

She gave Harris a light kiss on the cheek. This time, he did not object.

'Come on,' he said. 'Let's get inside.'

Once in the property, he watched as George and Esther walked down the stairs and followed them into the living room, where Gallagher had taken up a position by the window, his eyes scanning the hillside for signs of movement. The Matthewses looked tired and stressed.

'Sleep well?' asked the inspector.

Esther gave him a sour look. George said nothing.

'Here,' said Harris, handing him the newspaper. 'Thought you would like to see what the *Roxham Herald* has had to say about the shooting.'

'Like that will make me feel better,' said Matthews.

He sat down and scanned the front page, which was adorned by a large headline that said "Man dead in suspected accidental shooting" alongside a picture of police cars parked on Hewby Moor. Harris nodded his approval at the headline; the right message had been communicated by the press office. Matthews tapped the page.

'But you know that's not true,' he said.

'A little ruse, George,' said Harris. 'We can't risk anyone thinking that we have worked out what's really happening. Suffice to say, I'll have to do a lot of explaining when this is all over. It's going to cost me a few bottles of whisky, I suspect.'

Matthews turned over onto page three of the *Herald*, which featured a large photograph of Henry Masterson lifted from the newspaper's archives and taken at a country fair. It was accompanied by a caption explaining how the shooting had happened on his land.

'Now there's a face I recognise,' said Matthews. 'I've seen him with Stuart Davis. In Manchester. Jago was there as well.'

Harris walked across, looked over his shoulder and frowned as he stared at the image.

'What?' he said. 'Lynton Jago knows Henry Masterson? Are you sure about that?'

The inspector glanced at Gallagher, who walked over, glanced at the newspaper and looked at his boss in alarm. We've got the wrong man, said his expression. Harris felt a knot form in his stomach; taking Masterson into his confidence had been a mistake, after all. He had backed his instincts and jeopardised everything as a result. Had made the kind of schoolboy error he was constantly lecturing young detectives about. The inspector closed his eyes; he dreaded to think what Ged Rutherford would say when he found out.

'No,' said Matthews. He pointed to a man standing in the background of the picture. 'Him. He came to see Stuart. They were going for a drink. I got the impression that they had known each other for years.'

Harris peered closer into the face of Harry Groves. He relaxed and the knot in his stomach vanished.

'They certainly have,' he murmured. 'And old loyalties, it would seem, die hard.'

* * *

It was approaching 3:00pm when the gunman guided his car off the main valley road and headed along the rough track that led him to a spot behind a rocky outcrop, where he parked up. When he was satisfied that the vehicle was hidden from the road, he cut the engine, got out and opened the boot, from which he removed a rifle that he slung over his shoulder. He closed the boot and went back into the front seat where he removed a handgun from the glove compartment. After glancing around to double-check that no one was present, he locked the car and began to walk with a steady step in the direction of the cottage.

* * *

Shortly after 2:30pm, the Speedwagonz truck driver looked at the road sign. Calais 10 kilometres. The driver smiled – clear run.

Chapter twenty-five

It was approaching 4:00pm and the afternoon heat was beginning to dissipate as, having walked through the fields for less than an hour, the gunman first caught a glimpse of the cottage in the distance through a band of trees. Having made his way through the woodland, he emerged on the other side and lifted his binoculars to his eyes. He stood and surveyed the cottage for a few moments, seeking signs of movement.

Content that he had not been spotted, he slid the rifle from his shoulder, crouched down, lifted the sight to his eye and looked at the cottage again, this time honing in on the living room window. He had a good view. All it needed was one mistake, for George Matthews to pass unwittingly across the window, and with one shot the job would be done. He would not know what had hit him and, by the time police had arrived at the remote spot, he would be well on his way out of the valley. He'd already identified a C-road that was ideal for his escape.

The gunman gave a grunt of satisfaction and slipped onto his stomach. He made sure that the gun was resting comfortably in the crook of his arm and settled down to wait in the late afternoon sunshine.

* * *

It was just after 4:30pm when Moira Groves left the estate agents where she worked and walked through the town centre streets towards the marketplace, where she had parked her car that morning. Halfway across the square, she noticed two women approaching. Moira recognised one of them as Gillian Roberts. She did not recognise the young woman with her but assumed that she was also a police officer.

Something stirred deep within her, a sense of fear mixed with an intense feeling of resignation. Although she had been avoiding the thought, she had known that the police would come for her eventually and she felt a sudden wave of relief that finally she needed to carry the burden no longer.

'I wondered when you'd come to see me,' she said as the detectives approached.

'Then you'll know what it's about,' said Roberts. 'We think that you can assist us with our inquiries into the death of Geoff Morden. Will you come back to the station with us, please, Moira?'

Moira nodded. Roberts glanced at Sally Orr, who took Moira gently by the arm. Tears glistened in Moira's eyes as she allowed the young constable to lead her away.

* * *

Back on the hillside, the gunman had been waiting for twenty minutes but George Matthews had not appeared. Not that he minded. Not yet anyway. Patience had always been the name of the game in his line of work and there was time enough. Matthews would make a mistake sooner rather than later. Everyone dropped their guard in the end and, when they did, the gunman would squeeze the trigger and the job would be done.

* * *

Matty Gallagher and Alistair Marshall had been sitting in their car outside the Groves' home for twenty-five minutes when the call came on the sergeant's mobile.

'We've got her,' said Roberts' voice.

'OK,' said Gallagher.

The detectives got out of the car and walked over to the terraced house. The sergeant knocked on the door.

'Harry Groves,' said Gallagher as the door swung open. He showed the startled man his warrant card. 'I am arresting you on suspicion of conspiracy to murder Geoff Morden and conspiracy to murder George Matthews.'

Groves closed his eyes.

* * *

So intense was the gunman's focus on the cottage that he did not hear the soft tread of someone approaching on the soft carpet of pine needles behind him.

'Drop the weapon,' said a voice. 'Armed police.'

The gunman gave a cry of alarm and whirled round to see Jack Harris standing in among the trees. He was wearing a Kevlar vest and standing next to him was Davy Morrison, training his firearm on the man. The gunman lifted his rifle.

'Drop it!' said Harris with urgency in his voice.

The gunman hesitated then continued to lift the rifle until it pointed at the detective. He met the inspector's gaze, gave a slight smile and made as if to squeeze the trigger. The shot reverberated around the valley. When the sound had died away, Davy Morrison looked at the body lying on the ground with blood welling from a chest wound. The colour had drained from his face.

'Thirteen years in the job and I've never killed a man,' he said quietly.

'You never get used to it. I didn't.'

The inspector reached for the radio clipped to his belt.

'This is DCI Harris,' he said. 'Target acquired. Stand down.'

All across the hillside, armed officers emerged from their hiding places behind walls and boulders and in among trees and began to converge on the cottage.

Chapter twenty-six

'So, when did Harry find out about you and Geoff?' asked Gillian Roberts. The detective inspector looked across the interview room table at Moira Groves, who had been crying and was now sitting with her head bowed. 'Did you tell him?'

'No.' The voice was barely audible.

'Then how did he find out?'

Moira hesitated.

'Best to tell us everything, lovey,' said Roberts. She glanced at Sally Orr, who was sitting next to her, taking notes. 'Your husband is in trouble enough without you trying to conceal things from us, isn't that right, Constable?'

'Yes, ma'am. Best that we know everything.'

Moira thought for a moment and decided to unburden herself.

'This is difficult,' she said.

'It always is,' said Roberts. 'So, if you didn't tell Harry about the affair, how come he found out?'

'He saw me coming out of the house in Tenter Street a few nights ago,' said Moira. 'I didn't think he'd seen me at first, we'd been really careful, but I think he might have been looking for me. I had said I was at a friend's but he rang her up and I don't think he believed her when she said I'd just left. He didn't say anything when I got home. It was only two days later that he told me that he knew.'

'How long had the relationship been going on?' asked Roberts.

'Pretty much since Geoff came back to Levton Bridge. We'd had a thing for each other at college. Geoff was my first big love. We got together not long after Jack left to join the Army.' Moira gave a slight smile. 'I think I offered Geoff more interesting opportunities than egg collecting.'

'So how come you ended up with Harry instead?' asked Roberts.

'Me and Geoff lost touch when he left Levton Bridge. I never forgot him, though. I know what people said about him but he was a lot different once you got to know him.'

'So how did the relationship begin this time round?' asked Orr.

'We met in the street one afternoon. I didn't even know that he was back in town. Things went from there. Me and Harry have not been happy for years – marriage of convenience you might say. We've been sleeping in separate beds for as long as I can remember. Meeting Geoff again changed everything.' Moira's face assumed a far-off expression. 'We realised that we still had feelings for each other.'

'When did you know that Harry might have been involved in his murder?' asked the detective inspector.

'Not until you approached me this afternoon, and even now I'm not sure. I'd thought about it a couple of times but didn't believe it.'

'Really?' said Roberts. She was unable to conceal the surprise in her voice. 'Harry finds out about your affair and the next thing you know Geoff is dead? Doesn't that strike you as a bit of a coincidence?'

'Yes, but all the news reports said it was an accident so I was thinking how lucky Harry had been that the bullet missed him. I was thinking that it could have been him lying dead there.'

'Somehow, I don't think that was Harry's plan,' said Roberts. 'I think he intended all along that Geoff would be killed.'

'I'm still not sure I can believe that of him,' said Moira. 'Not Harry.'

'Believe it, lovey. He's been involved in some very heavy goings-on, has your husband.'

Moira looked at the detective inspector's sombre expression for a few moments then glanced at Orr, who nodded. Moira shook her head.

'You think you know someone,' she said.

'I'm sure your husband thought the same when he found out about your affair,' said Roberts.

'He probably half-expected it. It was Harry's biggest fear. That Geoff would come back one day. Him with all that money and the new cars and building a big new house. Harry always believed that he was no competition for someone like that.'

Silence settled on the room for a few moments then Moira turned her dark eyes on the detective inspector.

'Is Geoff dead because of me?' she asked quietly. 'Do you think I hold some responsibility for what happened?'

'Only you can answer that one,' said Roberts.

* * *

Jack Harris arrived back at Levton Bridge Police Station at 6:30pm to a CID squad room that was a hive of activity. He immediately headed for Roberts and Gallagher, who were sitting at a desk in the corner, comparing notes while drinking from mugs of tea laced with sugar for additional energy as the lack of sleep caught up with them. Scoot and Archie were curled up beneath a nearby radiator. Harris dragged a seat over, sat down wearily and closed his eyes.

'You OK?' asked Gallagher.

'Yeah,' said Harris. He opened his eyes. 'Just tired.'

'I know what you mean,' said Gallagher. 'I'm knackered. How's Davy Morrison?'

'Really cut up about having to kill the guy. Do we know who he was?'

'We sure do.' Gallagher held up a computer print-out. 'This came in from Interpol. They matched his fingerprints.'

'Interpol?'

'Yeah.' Gallagher slid the document across the desk so that the inspector could see a grainy image that Harris recognised as the man from the copse. 'If Davy's feeling bad, he can stop worrying. Turns out that he's one Michel Lefevre, a Frenchman. Believed to have been based in Paris. A real pro.'

Harris thought back to the moment the two men had exchanged glances in the copse shortly before Morrison fired. Having reflected on the event during the drive back to Levton Bridge, Harris had become convinced that Lefevre knew that he was about to be killed. It was almost as if he had chosen death ahead of the inevitable lengthy prison sentence that awaited him.

'What else do we know about him?' asked Harris.

'There's intelligence suggesting that he has been operating in the UK for more than ten years but nothing definite,' said Gallagher. 'Jago clearly knew him. There are also outstanding warrants for Lefevre's arrest in at least four European countries.'

'Contract killings?'

'Interpol reckon so. The victims were all involved in organised crime. Ballistics can't link the guns used in those killings to our incidents, but they can say that the gun that Lefevre had with him when he died was the one that killed Geoff Morden. I tell you, guv, Davy did the world a favour putting a bullet into him.'

'I'm sure the inquiry will take that into account.'

'He'll be OK, though, won't he?' said Gallagher. 'I mean, from what I hear, he had no option.'

'Yeah, I think so. He did save my life. That's another bottle of whisky I owe.' Harris stood up. 'Anything I need to know before we interview Harry Groves?'

'He definitely knew about the affair,' said Roberts.

'OK. You sit in with me on the interview then. Come on, let's see what he has got to say for himself.'

* * *

A few minutes later, the two detectives were sitting in the interview room, looking across the desk at Groves and his solicitor, a slim, balding man in his fifties.

'So, Harry,' said Harris, 'when did you decide that Geoff Morden had to die? When you saw Moira coming out of his house?'

'Who says I decided anything?' said Groves defiantly. 'You can't pin anything on me. After all, I was the one sitting next to him when he was shot, remember. How on earth could I have killed him?'

Harris did not reply but instead glanced at a sheet of paper lying on the desk. He did not speak for the best part of a minute, appearing to be fascinated by the contents, his lips moving silently as he read and ran his finger down the page. Groves watched him with a rising sense of anxiety. Eventually, as the tension grew in the room, Harris looked across at Roberts.

'It's interesting stuff, isn't it?' he said.

'Pretty damning, I would say.'

'What is it?' Groves reached across the table to grasp the piece of paper but Harris moved to stop him. The inspector's grip was firm and Groves winced and withdrew his hand.

'This,' said Harris, 'is your mobile phone record for the past few days. Do you know what it tells us?'

Groves did not reply.

'Well, I'll refresh your memory then,' said Harris. 'It says that you have been in regular contact with Stuart Davis.'

'I haven't seen Stuart for years,' said Groves. He sat back and crossed his arms. 'Not since we were kids. And you can't prove otherwise.'

'Oh, but we can. You met him in Manchester last year. We have a witness.'

'Well, whoever said that is lying and you should know better than to–'

'Don't play games with me!' snapped Harris. His irritation was fuelled by lack of sleep. 'We know that you and Stuart have been in regular contact and we know that Stuart works for Lynton Jago.'

'Who's he?'

'I think you know exactly who he is,' said Harris.

'So, what if I do?' said Groves. He was more wary now. 'That proves nothing, does it?'

'It proves conspiracy, if nothing else,' said Roberts.

Groves looked at his solicitor.

'Is she right?' he asked.

'It could well be the case,' said the lawyer.

'Well, I don't know what you are talking about,' said Groves. He turned back to the detectives. 'You've got nothing on me.'

'Let me lay it out for you, then,' said Harris. 'This afternoon, a gunman was shot dead by a police officer near the cottage which we think you discovered was being used to hold a man who is prepared to give evidence against Lynton Jago.'

The colour drained from Groves' face.

'What's more,' said Harris, 'our ballistics people have proved that his gun was the one that killed Geoff Murden.'

'Yes, but that does not mean that I had anything to do with it, does it?' said Groves. However, his voice lacked conviction.

Harris tapped the list of phone numbers.

'No, but this does,' he said. 'This proves everything. Time to come clean, Harry.'

Groves thought for a few moments.

'What will happen to me if I do?' he asked. He looked at his lawyer again. 'I mean, they still can't prove that I knew what was going to happen to Geoff, can they?'

'I think I'd rather like to hear what the chief inspector has to say before I answer,' said the solicitor.

'In which case, let me tell you what we think,' said Harris. 'We think that your client was furious when he found out that Geoff Morden was having an affair with his wife.'

'It was the thing he dreaded more than anything else, according to Moira,' said Roberts.

'We also think,' said Harris, 'that your client knew that Geoff was into some pretty heavy criminal activities and that he saw his opportunity to get rid of him.'

He looked at Groves.

'How am I doing so far?' he asked.

Groves said nothing but the sick expression on his face was answer enough.

'What I don't know,' said the DCI, 'is how you found out that Geoff was tied up with organised crime in the first place. It's hardly the kind of thing you pop into casual conversation, is it? Come on, Harry, time to tell us the truth about what happened.'

Groves sighed.

'OK, OK,' he said. 'I found out when we were drinking whisky up at the nest one night. A couple of days before I found out about the affair. We'd had a bit too much and suddenly Geoff was saying that he was involved with this Lynton Jago fellow and that Stuart was involved as well. He said he was looking for a way to get out. That he was thinking about telling you what he knew to see if you could get him out of trouble.'

The words were coming out rapidly now as Harry Groves unburdened himself.

'He was really frightened,' said Groves. 'He said that Jago had had people killed before for informing on him and that maybe you could offer him protection. Next morning, he was horrified by what he had said, said he'd been drunk, and begged me not to tell anyone. I agreed.'

'But then you found out about the affair?' said Harris. 'And saw a way of getting him out of the picture?'

'I still had Stuart's number from when we met up for a drink so I told him what Geoff had said. I didn't know any of the details but I didn't really need them. Stuart said to leave it to him. I knew I'd made a mistake immediately. I wasn't thinking straight.'

'Seems like you were thinking very clearly,' said Harris. He was struggling to conceal the disgust from his voice. 'You as good as put the rifle in the gunman's hand. If it hadn't been for you, Geoff Morden might still be alive.'

'Think I care?' hissed Groves. His sudden venom startled the detectives. 'I hated the flash bastard. Always banging on about his new house and how much money his company is worth and boasting about having a new car every six months. And then to think about him and Moira… his hands all over her…'

Groves' voice tailed off as he sought to regain his composure. The detectives allowed the silence to lengthen.

'But none of this makes me guilty of murder, does it?' he said when the rage had passed. 'Besides, I rang Stuart twice to ask him to ignore what I had said. What else could I have done?'

'You could have told Geoff that he was in danger,' said Roberts. 'Tipped him off. Or told us.'

'And end up being charged with conspiracy to murder?' Groves shook his head. 'I couldn't take the risk.'

'But you didn't mind Geoff taking the risk, did you?' said Harris. 'Whose idea was it to make his death look like an accident?'

'Stuart's. After I told him about the nest, he said it was ideal. Said you'd assume it was someone trying to kill the birds. Said no one would think to connect it with him and Lynton Jago.'

'And what about George Matthews?' asked Harris. 'How come you set out to find him?'

'Stuart told me to do it. I didn't want to but he said that if I didn't co-operate, they could just as easily have me killed as well. I'd seen what they'd done to Geoff and there was no way I was going to argue.'

Harris shook his head.

'What a mess,' he said. He glanced up at the wall clock. Time was advancing. The truck would already be back in the UK. 'How was Davis to be told that Matthews had been killed? Was Lefevre going to ring him?'

'No, they kept phone contact to a minimum. Stuart said they'd know when they heard about it on the news.'

'Gillian,' said Harris, turning to the detective inspector. 'Get hold of the press office, will you? Tell them we want to issue a press release.'

* * *

Harris did not get home until approaching midnight and, having taken the dogs for a late walk across the fields by torchlight, he had just returned to the cottage and slumped into his armchair with a glass of whisky when his mobile rang. He sighed.

'What now?' he said. He noted the call was from Susan Peters.

He took the call. She sounded worried.

'Jack,' she said. 'I've just had Ged Rutherford on. They think Jago's people were spooked by a couple of patrol cars near the Speedwagonz depot earlier tonight – nothing to do with the surveillance – and the truck has bypassed Manchester and is heading towards your area.'

Harris sat bolt upright.

'Our area?' he said.

'Yes, we've intercepted a communication that suggests they are planning to unload the firearms at a truck stop on the M6. It's pretty remote but the map says that it's level with Levton Bridge.'

'Yeah, I know it,' said Harris. 'Speedwagonz drivers sometimes park up there overnight.'

'Well, that's where it's going to happen. Gary Nesbitt and Linda Morden are already heading north in a van.'

'Linda?'

'Apparently so,' said Peters.

'You think you know someone, eh?'

'Can you handle something this big, Jack? Will you need me to send some of Ged's people?'

Harris held his whisky up and beamed as he appreciated the way it glinted in the glow from the table lamp.

'Oh, I think we'll be alright,' he said.

He ended the call but, before he could contact the firearms unit, his phone rang again. Seeing it was Rutherford, he smiled and took the call.

'Ged,' he said. 'Now what do you want, I wonder?'

'I take it you're loving this, you bastard?' growled Rutherford.

'Who, me?' Harris took a sip of whisky. 'Nothing could be further from the truth.'

'Don't try it on, Jack. I know you of old, remember. Anyway, wondered if you wanted any help with the truck?'

'Susan asked me that as well but, no, I think we'll be OK, Ged. I mean, as you yourself said, it's down to whichever force covers the area, isn't it? No, we'll be fine – as long as there aren't too many sheep, of course.'

'Funny man,' said Rutherford and ended the call

Harris took another sip of whisky.

'And Matty says I can't do politics,' he said.

Chapter twenty-seven

The night was at its deepest when the lorry's headlights pierced the darkness, glimpsed initially by the waiting detectives as faint gleams picking their way between the shadowy shapes of the northern hills. The lights grew stronger as the vehicle neared the truck stop and the officers heard the dull throb of its engine, carried on the still air as it moved onto the northbound slip road and crossed the bridge over the motorway before rumbling down into the lorry park. Sitting in an unmarked van on the edge of the park, partially hidden by the toilet block, Harris and Gallagher exchanged glances.

'Looks like MI5 were right,' said the sergeant. 'And it's all ours.'

'Looks like it,' said Harris. 'Ged Rutherford *will* be pleased.'

'Yeah, I'm sure.'

The detectives had arrived at the lorry park an hour and a half previously, accompanied by a team of uniformed officers, many of them armed. On arrival, the officers had quickly woken the drivers sleeping in their cabs before they had a chance to issue a warning over the airwaves, should the brotherhood of the road so tempt them. The drivers had been quickly removed from the site and were being held at Levton Bridge Police Station until the operation was completed.

Harris and Gallagher shrank down in their seats as the lorry juddered to a halt with a hissing of its brakes and, from their vantage point, the detectives could see the driver illuminated by an internal light in the cab as he sat back in his seat to ease his aching limbs after his long drive.

'Now for the others,' said Harris.

A minute later, more headlights appeared in the distance, eventually revealing themselves as belonging to a white Transit van which also took the slip road and crossed the bridge into the lorry park. The van driver flashed its lights twice and drove over to the truck, where it pulled to a halt. Two figures got out. Harris instantly recognised them as Linda Morden and Gary Nesbitt.

'Ah, Linda, Linda, Linda,' said the inspector in a quiet voice. 'She sure had me fooled.'

'It seems like Geoff was betrayed by everyone,' said Gallagher. 'The DI was right. It usually *is* the person closest to you, isn't it? Hang on, wasn't she the one that put us onto Stuart Davis in the first place?'

'It was indeed. I look forward to her explanation.'

They watched as the lorry driver climbed down from his cab and stood chatting to the new arrivals for a few moments before opening the rear of his truck and clambering inside. As he did so, another set of headlights appeared in the distance and, after a few minutes, a black BMW with tinted windows made the same journey over the motorway bridge and down into the lorry park where it drew to a halt beside the lorry. Two men got out. Harris did not recognise the one who emerged from the passenger seat but he knew immediately the identity of the driver.

'Stuart Davis,' he said.

'Is the other guy Jago?' asked Gallagher.

'No, he'll not get his hands dirty. That's how he has kept himself out of prison all these years. There's time enough for him, though.'

The detectives watched with increasing eagerness as Davis had a brief conversation with Linda Morden then clambered up into the back of the lorry. Nesbitt backed the van up to the vehicle, got out and opened the rear doors. The truck driver and Davis emerged from the lorry, struggling with a heavy wooden crate, which the watching detectives could see was adorned with a label depicting tins of fruit.

'Strike one to MI5,' said Harris. He reached for the car's radio. 'All units, go, go. That's all units go, go.'

Engines fired up and headlights cut through the darkness as several unmarked cars appeared at speed from behind the parked lorries, with their tyres squealing. They slewed to a halt next to the truck amid a shower of gravel and armed officers jumped out of the vehicles, hollering warnings. Startled, Nesbitt and the truck driver threw up their hands immediately but the man who had arrived with Stuart Davis gave a roar of anger and turned to flee.

'Armed police!' shouted an officer as he began to run. 'Stand still or I *will* shoot!'

The man hesitated then turned and held up his hands in surrender, resignation written large across his face. As officers secured him, Harris saw Stuart Davis running across the lorry park and gave chase. Davis reached the edge of the park first and turned to face Harris. He was about to shout something at the inspector when a shape hurtled out of the darkness and sent him crashing to the ground with an agonised yell as his shoulder hit the floor, sending shards of pain through his arm. By the time Harris had arrived, Matty Gallagher had twisted his quarry's arms behind his back and hauled him roughly to his feet.

'This reminds me of one time when I was in the Met,' said Gallagher with an impish grin on his face.

Harris roared with laughter and slapped the sergeant heartily on the shoulder.

'You can tell that story as many times as you like, Matty lad,' he said. Harris gave Davis a playful punch on the arm and beamed as the prisoner cried out in pain again. 'Eh, Stuart?'

Gallagher led Davis over to the others, the prisoner still rubbing his throbbing arm. One of the firearms officers had already handcuffed Linda's arms behind her back.

'And what's your game?' asked Harris. He gestured to the officers who were removing the first of the guns from the crate. 'First you put us onto Stuart then we find you here.'

Davis and Nesbitt stared at her, aghast.

'You did what?' said Nesbitt.

'All I did was tell them about Dad meeting Stuart for a drink.' She looked at Harris. 'I didn't know the significance of it then, Jack. You have to believe me about that. I only found out what's been happening when Gary told me on the way back to Manchester this afternoon. I'll tell you everything I know.'

'Everything?' said Harris.

'Everything.'

'We'll have you for this, you bitch,' rasped Davis. He struggled to free himself from Gallagher's grip but gave up after a few moments as the hold remained unrelenting. 'There ain't nowhere you can hide.'

'You shouldn't have killed my father,' said Linda quietly. Her eyes glistened with tears.

Harris looked at Nesbitt.

'And you,' he said. 'How come you're involved?'

'You don't say no to Lynton Jago,' replied Nesbitt. 'Geoff found that out the hard way. Besides, it's nothing to do with us how they use the guns. It's not our responsibility, is it?'

'There's too many people who have said that over the past twenty-four hours,' said Harris. 'And it won't make a judge any less sympathetic.'

Nesbitt thought for a moment.

'What if I offer to help you as well?' he said.

Davis gave a snarl and struggled to get free again but Gallagher tightened his grip.

'Depends how you help us,' said Harris.

'I'm prepared to tell you what I know,' said Nesbitt. 'If you can guarantee that my wife and kids will be kept safe.'

'We'll find them, wherever you put them,' said Davis. 'You mark my words, you bastard!'

Harris looked at Gallagher.

'Get him out of my sight,' he said with a scowl. 'In fact, get them all out of my sight.'

Gallagher handed Davis over to one of the uniformed officers and the two detectives watched as all three prisoners were led away to the waiting police vans.

'So, Geoff was one of the good guys, after all,' said Gallagher when they were out of earshot.

'Once, maybe,' replied Harris. His mind went back to happy summer days as two young boys roamed the northern hills, dogs at their heels. 'I'm not sure anyone really comes out of this well, Matty lad.'

'Except us.'

Harris looked at the sergeant and smiled.

'Except us,' he said. 'How right you are, Matty lad.'

One of the armed officers walked across after placing Stuart Davis in one of the vans.

'He's changed his tune,' he said. 'Says he can see the way it's going and wants to do a deal as well. Everything he knows about Lynton Jago in return for protection.'

'Bloody hell,' said Gallagher. 'They're queuing up. Witness Protection will have to go into the housebuilding business at this rate!'

'Well, I just happen to know a plot of land that's available,' said Harris. 'And if they play their cards right, it could even have turrets.'

Gallagher nodded approvingly.

'Very good,' he said. 'Your sense of humour is coming on nicely. That's three jokes this year. My work here may soon be done.'

Harris allowed himself a smile then made a call on his mobile phone.

'Your people can go in,' he said.

* * *

Following the inspector's call to Susan Peters, things moved rapidly at several locations around the UK. Amid tearing timber and hollered warnings, armed officers knocked through front doors at a number of houses, surprising the sleeping occupants. Among the properties raided was a semi-detached house in a tree-lined suburb in Stevenage, which intelligence officers had identified as the home of the ringleader of the far-right group. Officers crashed through his front door and thundered up the stairs to the bedroom, where they found the young man in the act of heading for the window. As the armed officers entered the room, he whirled round, stared at their guns in horror and sat down heavily on the bed. Within seconds, and in a state of shock, he had been handcuffed.

One of the armed officers looked at the posters on the wall, read the hate-filled racist slogans, viewed the violent themes depicted in the images, glanced at the innocuous-looking young man sitting on the bed and shook his head

'I thought I'd seen everything,' he said.

* * *

An hour later, with the suspects well on their way to Levton Bridge, Harris and Gallagher were still at the lorry park, overseeing the search of the truck, which had already gleaned thirty weapons. The inspector's mobile phone rang.

'Well done,' said Susan Peters. 'Well done indeed.'

'Thank you. Team effort.'

'Talking of teamwork, I understand that you and Ged are going to pick up Jago later this morning?'

'Yeah, that's right,' said Harris. 'They've got him under surveillance but he'll not dare go anywhere. He'll try to wheedle his way out of it as usual. Not sure he'll manage it this time, though. Did everyone else get picked up alright?'

'Counter Terrorism picked up all our far-right friends, yes. They had absolutely no idea that we were onto them. There's already a couple on the fringe who are saying that it had all got out of hand and that they're prepared to give evidence against the others. We've saved a lot of lives tonight, Jack.'

'Excellent,' said Harris.

'You'll also be glad to know that the Kosovan police have just picked up your man at a flat in Pristina. They're interrogating him now. I wouldn't like to be in his shoes.'

Jack Harris thought back to the chill of that evening in the dank forest, to the bodies of the children lying in the clearing, to the appalled expressions on the faces of the soldiers who had discovered them. To the nightmares. He felt extremely tired and unable to find the words to reply.

Chapter twenty-eight

It was just gone 10:00am when Jack Harris and Ged Rutherford strode into the car showroom in Manchester and, waving aside the protestations from staff, walked up the stairs towards Lynton Jago's office. Scarface was waiting at the top, blocking their way. He leered at them and raised a hand as if to strike but Harris darted forward and slammed a fist deep into his solar plexus. Scarface grunted in pain as the air was driven from his lungs. As he doubled over, clutching his stomach, Harris flicked out a foot and sent him crashing down the stairs where he careered into the wall then lay still. Rutherford glanced down at the prostrate figure and gave Harris a wry smile.

'Same old Jack Harris, eh!' he said.

'So, sue me,' said Harris.

Rutherford gave a low laugh.

'I guess you have your uses,' he said.

They pushed their way into the office to find Lynton Jago sitting behind his desk. He looked relaxed. Confident.

'Gentlemen,' he said with a disarming smile. 'I have been expecting you, although I fear you have had a wasted journey.'

'I think not,' said Rutherford. He produced a set of handcuffs and prepared to utter the words he had long wanted to say. 'Lynton Jago, I am arresting you on suspicion of money laundering.'

A look of amusement flickered across Jago's face.

'You'll have to do better than that,' he said. 'Not now George Matthews is dead. It was him in that unfortunate shooting that they reported on the radio, wasn't it?'

'Now, where did you get that idea?' said Rutherford. He turned to Harris. 'George isn't dead, is he?'

'Not the last time I checked. In fact, the last thing I heard, he was having eggs and bacon for breakfast. Nope, it was some fellow called Michel Lefevre who died.'

Jago gave a start but recovered himself quickly.

'I've never heard of him,' he said.

'Tell it to the judge,' said Harris. 'Lynton Jago, I am arresting you in connection with the murder of Geoff Morden and the attempted murder of George Matthews.'

Jago gave a snort of derision.

'You'll never get any of that to stick,' he said.

'I'm not sure that Stuart Davis would agree,' said Harris with a cheery smile. 'If you can get a word in, that is. You can't stop him talking once he starts, can you? He's quite the chatterbox.'

The colour drained from Jago's face.

'And as for Linda Morden and Gary Nesbitt,' said Harris. He gave a half-smile. 'Well, let's just say that they're singing like birds.'

Jago closed his eyes.

'I told you I'd get you one day, you bastard,' said Harris, his voice hard-edged.

Rutherford looked at Harris and dangled the handcuffs.

'So, I guess you would like to do the honours?' he said.

Harris shook his head.

'No, it's fine,' he said. 'I think you've deserved this one, Ged. No, I'm going home to catch up on my sleep. Send him to Levton Bridge when you've finished with him, will you?'

And he walked from the room and down the stairs, leaving a surprised and delighted Rutherford to apply the cuffs and, a couple of minutes later, to lead a glowering Lynton Jago past the groaning figure of Scarface and out into morning sunshine that seemed to the DCI to be as bright as ever he could remember.

* * *

Several days later, Jack Harris and Henry Masterson were sitting on the terrace behind the house at the Hewby Moor Estate, sipping from glasses of whisky as they soaked up the early evening warmth and appreciated the way that the shadows were lengthening across the hills. The inspector's dogs were nosing around the garden.

'Thanks for the whisky,' said Masterson.

'Least I could do,' said Harris. 'I've got one for Bill as well.'

'The paper said that Harry Groves is going to plead not guilty,' said Masterson. 'Will he get off with it?'

Harris shrugged.

'Who knows?' he said. 'One for the jury. Let them work it out. The CPS seem to think that they can get him on conspiracy, if nothing else. Thank you for deciding not to press charges against Pete Guthrie. He appreciates it and so do I.'

'Well, what would it have achieved?' said Masterson.

'I take it you know that it won't stop him getting on your case about the hen harriers? Nor me, for that matter.'

'I am afraid that it's part of the rich fabric of rural life,' said Masterson. He took a sip of whisky. 'Besides, a court case would only have been bad for business, especially if it had happened in the lead up to the Glorious Twelfth. The last thing I want is a load of cancellations because folks are worried that some crazy will whack them over the head with a baseball bat.'

Harris gave him a sly look.

'No gangsters on the guest list this year, I hope?' he said.

'No, no gangsters.' Masterson was silent for a few moments. 'You never really thought that me and Bill were involved in the murder, did you, Jack? I mean, not *really*?'

'Not really,' said the inspector. 'Although there was the odd moment when I did wonder. Some of your business associates do leave something to be desired, might I suggest.'

'I guess.'

'And Bill Harding didn't exactly help when he tried to warn off Alison Butterfield,' said Harris. 'That wasn't the brightest of moves.'

'He was just trying to protect the business and, at the end of the day, that's all it's about. Money in the bank.'

Harris was about to reply when a dark shape caught his attention over the far side of the moor. The two men watched for a few minutes until it revealed itself as a bird of prey swooping low over the heather. A broad smile worked its way across the inspector's face.

'Unless I am very much mistaken,' he said, 'that is a juvenile hen harrier out searching for a spot of supper. Who knows, it might even be on for a spot of red grouse. What do you think, Henry?'

Masterson sighed.

'I am afraid, my dear inspector,' he said, 'that you may well be right.'

Harris raised the glass to his lips.

'Cheers,' he said.

THE END

List of Characters

Levton Bridge Police:

Superintendent Philip Curtis – divisional commander
Detective Chief Inspector Jack Harris
Detective Inspector Gillian Roberts
Inspector Charlie Gates
Detective Sergeant Matty Gallagher
Detective Constable Alison Butterfield
PC Leslie Jardine
Detective Constable Alistair Marshall
PC Davy Morrison – Firearms Unit
Detective Constable Sally Orr

Other police officers:

Detective Chief Inspector Ged Rutherford, Head of Greater Manchester Police Organised Crime Unit
Detective Inspector Jenny Armannsson, Head of Greater Manchester Police (GMP) Fraud Squad
Detective Sergeant Gerry Bayliss, Greater Manchester Police Organised Crime Unit
PC Graham Leckie – intelligence officer with Greater Manchester Police

Other characters:

Bob Crowther – Head of Levton Bridge Mountain Rescue Team
Stuart Davis – a gangster
Des – property letting agency owner
Doc – Home Office pathologist
Harry Groves – amateur ornithologist
Moira Groves – his wife
Pete Guthrie – amateur ornithologist
Bill Harding – manager of the Hewby Manor Estate
Lynton Jago – gangster
Bernard Joffey – general manager of The Hillview Hotel
Michel Lefevre – professional hitman
Henry Masterson – owner of the Hewby Manor Estate
George Matthews – financial advisor
Esther Matthews – his wife
Geoff Morden – amateur ornithologist and owner of haulage company Speedwagonz
Linda Morden – Geoff's daughter
Gary Nesbitt – financial director of Speedwagonz
Susan Peters – MI5 officer
Scarface – gangster

If you enjoyed this book, please let others know by leaving a quick review on Amazon. Also, if you spot anything untoward in the paperback, get in touch. We strive for the best quality and appreciate reader feedback.

editor@thebookfolks.com

www.thebookfolks.com

ALSO BY JOHN DEAN

In this series:

Dead Hill (Book 1)
The Vixen's Scream (Book 2)
To Die Alone (Book 3)
To Honour the Dead (Book 4)
Thou Shalt Kill (Book 5)
Error of Judgement (Book 6)
The Killing Line (Book 7)

In the DCI John Blizzard series:

The Long Dead
Strange Little Girl
The Railway Man
The Secrets Man
A Breach of Trust
Death List
A Flicker in the Night
The Latch Man

Printed in Great Britain
by Amazon

71697287R00118